Crash Diet

Also by Jill McCorkle

CRASH DIET

Stories

by Jill McCorkle

Algonquin Books of Chapel Hill

1992

Published by
Algonquin Books of Chapel Hill
Post Office Box 2225
Chapel Hill, North Carolina 27515-2225
a division of
Workman Publishing Company, Inc.
708 Broadway
New York, New York 10003
© 1992 by Jill McCorkle.
Design by Molly Renda.

This is a work of fiction. While, as in all fiction, the literary percep-
tions and insights are based on experience, all names, characters,
places, and incidents are either products of the author's imagination
or are used fictitiously. No reference to any real person is intended or
should be inferred.

The author wishes to extend a long overdue thanks to Ann Crowther,
Mimi Fountain, Bettye Dew, Liz Darhansoff, Susan Cobb, and Linda
Dunn for their invaluable assistance and friendship. And, as always,
thanks to Louis Rubin, Rhoda and David Shapiro, Melba and John
McCorkle, Dan and Claudia.

Some of the stories originally appeared, sometimes in slightly different versions, in the following periodicals, to whose editors grateful
acknowledgment is made: "The First Union Blues" in *Southern Magazine*, "Crash Diet" in *Cosmopolitan*, "Waiting for Hard Times to End"
and "Comparison Shopping" in *The Southern Review*, "Departures"
in *Atlantic Monthly*, "Gold Mine" in *The Greensboro Review*, "Words
Gone Bad" in *New Virginia Review*, "Man Watcher" in *The Crescent Review*, and "Carnival Lights" in *Seventeen*. Two stories also
appeared in *New Stories from the South*.

Library of Congress Cataloging-in-Publication Data
McCorkle, Jill, 1958–
    Crash diet : stories / Jill McCorkle.—1st ed.
        p.   cm.
    ISBN 0-945575-75-0
    1. Women—Southern States—Fiction.   I. Title.
PS3563.C3444C7   1992
813'.54—dc20   91-34313 CIP

10 9 8 7 6 5 4 3 2 1

First Edition

For Jan Gane and Cathy Caldwell,
who have listened patiently to my stories for years.

And for Shannon Ravenel,
without whose encouragement they would
never have been written.

Contents

Crash Diet

Crash Diet

Kenneth left me on a Monday morning before I'd even had the chance to mousse my hair, and I just stood there at the picture window with the drapes swung back and watched him get into that flashy red Mazda, which I didn't want him to get anyway, and drive away down Marnier Street, and make a right onto Seagrams. That's another thing I didn't want, to live in a subdivision where all the streets are named after some kind of liquor. But Kenneth thought that was cute because he runs a bartending school, which is where he met Lydia to begin with.

"I'll come back for the rest of my things," he said, and I wondered just what he meant by that. What was his and what was mine?

"Where are you going to live, in a pup tent?" I asked and

1

took the towel off of my head. I have the kind of hair that will dry right into big clumps of frosted-looking thread if I don't comb it out fast. Once, well before I met Kenneth at the Holiday Inn lounge where he was giving drink-mixing lessons to the staff, I wrote a personal ad and described myself as having angel hair, knowing full well that whoever read it would picture flowing blond curls, when what I really meant was the stuff that you put on a Christmas tree or use to insulate your house. I also said I was average size, which at the time I was.

"I'm moving in with Lydia," he said in his snappy, matter-of-fact way, like I had just trespassed on his farmland. Lydia. It had been going on for a year and a half though I had only known of it for six weeks. *LYDIA*, a name so old-sounding even my grandmother wouldn't have touched it.

"Well, give her my best," I said like you might say to a child who is threatening to run away from home. "Send me a postcard," I said and laughed, though I already felt myself nearing a crack, like I might fall right into it, a big dark crack, me and five years of Kenneth and liquor streets and the microwave oven that I'd just bought to celebrate our five years of marriage and the fact that I had finally started losing some of the weight that I had put on during the first two years.

"Why did you do this?" he asked when he came home that day smelling of coconut because he had been teaching piña coladas, and approached that microwave oven that I had tied up in red ribbon.

"It's our anniversary," I said and told him that he was making me so hungry for macaroons or those Hostess Sno-balls with all that pink coconut. I'd lost thirty pounds by that time and needed to lose only ten more and they were going to take my "after" picture and put me on the wall of the Diet Center along with all the other warriors (that's what they called us) who had conquered fat.

"But this is a big investment," Kenneth said and picked up the warranty. Five years, and he stared at that like it had struck some chord in his brain that was high-pitched and off-key. Five years, that's how long it had been since we honeymooned down at Sea Island, Georgia, and drank dai-quiris that Kenneth said didn't have enough rum and ate all kinds of wonderful food that Kenneth didn't monitor going down my throat like he came to do later.

"Well, sure it's an investment," I told him. "Like a marriage."

"Guaranteed for five years," he said and then got all choked up, tried to talk but cried instead, and I knew something wasn't right. I sat up half the night waiting for him to say something. *Happy anniversary, You sure do look good these days*, anything. It must have been about two A.M. when I got out of him the name Lydia, and I didn't do a thing but get up and out of that bed and start working on the mold that wedges in between those tiles in the shower stall. That's what I do when I get upset because it's hard to eat while scrubbing and because there's always mold to be found if you look for it.

"You'll have to cross that bridge when you come to it," my mama always said, and when I saw Kenneth make that right turn onto Seagrams, I knew I was crossing it right then. I had two choices: I could go back to bed or I could do something. I have never been one to climb back into the bed after it's been made, so I got busy. I moussed my hair and got dressed, and I went to my pocketbook and got out the title to that Mazda that had both our names on it. I poured a glass of wine, since it was summer vacation from teaching sixth grade, painted my toenails, and then, in the most careful way, I wrote in Kenneth's handwriting that I (Kenneth I. Barkley) gave full ownership of the Mazda to Sandra White Barkley, and then I signed his name. Even Kenneth couldn't have told that it wasn't his signature; that's just how well I forged. I finished my wine, got dressed, and went over to my friend Paula's house to get it notarized.

"Why are you doing this?" Paula asked me. She was standing there in her bathrobe, and I could hear some movement in the back where her bedroom was. I didn't know if she meant why was I stopping by her house unannounced or why I was changing the title on the car. I know it's rude to stop by a person's house unannounced and hated to admit I had done it, so I just focused on the title. Sometimes I can focus so well on things and other times I can't at all.

"Kenneth and I are separating and I get the Mazda," I told her.

"When did this happen?" Paula asked, and·glanced over her shoulder to that cracked bedroom door.

"About two hours ago," I told her and sat down on the sofa. Paula just kept standing there like she didn't know what to do, like she could have killed me for just coming in and having a seat in the middle of her activities, but I didn't focus on that. "Just put your stamp on it and I'll be going." I held that title and piece of paper out to her, and she stared down at it and shook her head back and forth. "Did Kenneth write this?" she asked me, like my reputation might not be the best.

"Haven't I been through enough this morning?" I asked her and worked some tears into my eyes. "What kind of friend questions such a thing?"

"I'm sorry, Sandra," she said, her face as pink as her bath-robe. "I have to ask this sort of thing. I'll be right back." She went down the hall to her bedroom, and I got some candy corn out of her little dish shaped like a duck or some-thing in that family. I wedged the large ends up and over my front teeth so I had fangs like little kids always do at Halloween.

"Who was that?" I heard a man say, frustrated. I could

hear frustration in every syllable that carried out there to the living room, and then Paula said, "Shhh." When she came back with her little embosser, I had both front teeth covered in candy corn and grinned at her. She didn't laugh so I took them off my teeth and laid them on her coffee table. I don't eat sweets.

"I'm sorry I can't talk right now," Paula said. "You see . . ."

"What big eyes you have," I said and took my notarized paper right out of her hand. "Honey, go for it," I told her and pointed down the hall. "I'm doing just fine."

"I feel so guilty, though," Paula said, her hair all flat on one side from sleeping that way. "I feel like maybe you need to talk to somebody." That's what people always say when they feel like they should do something but have no intention of doing it, *I feel so bad*, or *If only*. I just laughed and told Paula I had to go to Motor Vehicles and take care of a piece of business and then I had to go to the police station and report a stolen car.

"What?" Paula asked, and her mouth fell open and she didn't even look over her shoulder when there were several frustrated and impatient knocks on her bedroom wall. "That's illegal."

"And you're my accomplice," I told her and walked on down the sidewalk and got into that old Ford Galaxy, which still smelled like the apples that Kenneth's grand-daddy used to keep in it to combat his cigar smoke. If there'd been a twenty-year-old apple to be found rolling around there under the front seat, I would've eaten it.

I didn't report the car, though. By the time I had driven by Lydia's house fourteen times—the first four of which the Mazda was out front and the other ten parked two blocks away behind the fish market (hidden, they thought)—I was too tired to talk to anybody so I just went home to bed. By ten o'clock, I'd had a full night's sleep so I got up, thawed some hamburger in the microwave, and made three pans of lasagna, which I then froze because mozzarella is not on my diet.

The next day, I was thinking about going to the grocery store because I didn't have a carrot in the house, but it was as if my blood was so slow I couldn't even put on a pair of socks. I felt like I had taken a handful of Valium but I hadn't. I checked the bottle there at the back of the medicine cabinet that was prescribed for Kenneth when he pulled his back lifting a case of Kahlúa about a year ago. The bottle was there with not a pill touched, so I didn't have an excuse to be found for this heaviness. "When you feel heavy, exercise!" we warriors say, so before my head could be turned toward something like cinnamon toast, I got dressed and did my Jane Fonda routine twice, scrubbed the gasoline spots from the driveway, and then drove to the Piggly Wiggly for some carrots. It felt good being in the car with the radio going, so I didn't get out at the Piggly

Wiggly but kept driving. I had never seen that rotating bar that is in a motel over in Clemmonsville, so I went there. It was not nearly as nice as Kenneth had made it sound; I couldn't even tell that I was moving at all, so I rode the glass elevator twice, and then checked into the motel across the street. It was a motel like I'd never seen, electric finger massages for a quarter and piped-in reggae. I liked it so much I stayed a week and ate coleslaw from Kentucky Fried Chicken. When I got home, I bought some carrots at the Piggly Wiggly.

"I was so worried about you!" my buddy Martha from the Diet Center said, and ran into my house. Martha is having a long hard time getting rid of her excess. "I was afraid you were binging."

"No, just took a little trip for my nerves," I told her, and she stood with her mouth wide open like she had seen Frankenstein. "Kenneth and I have split." Martha's mouth was still hanging open, which is part of her problem: oral, she's an oral person.

"Look at you," Martha said, and put her hands on my hips, squeezed on my bones there, love handles they're sometimes called if you've got somebody who loves them. "You've lost, Sandra."

"Well, Kenneth and I weren't right for each other, I guess."

"The hell with Kenneth," Martha said, her eyes filling

with tears. "You've lost more weight." Martha shook my hips until my teeth rattled. She is one of those people who her whole life has been told she has a pretty face. And she does, but it makes her mad for people to say it because she knows what they mean is that she's fat, and to ignore that fact they say what a pretty face she has. Anybody who's ever been overweight has had this happen. "I'm going to miss you at the meetings," Martha said, and looked like she was going to cry again. Martha is only thirty, just five years younger than me, but she looks older; the word is *matronly*, and it has a lot to do with the kind of clothes you have to wear if you're overweight. The mall here doesn't have an oversize shop.

I went to the beauty parlor and told them I wanted the works—treatments, facials, haircut, new shampoo, mousse, spray, curling wand. I spent a hundred and fifty dollars there, and then I went to Revco and bought every color of nail polish that they had, four different new colognes because they each represented a different mood, five boxes of Calgon in case I didn't get back to Revco for a while, all the Hawaiian Tropic products, including a sun visor and beach towel. I bought a hibachi and three bags of charcoal, a hammock, some barbecue tongs, an apron that says KISS THE COOK, and one of those inflatable pools so I could stretch out in the backyard in some water. I bought one of those rafts that will hold a canned drink in a little pocket, in case I should decide to walk down to the pool in our subdivision over on Tequila Circle. Summer was well under way, and I had to catch up on things. I bought a garden hose and a hoe and a rake, thinking I might relandscape my yard even though the subdivision doesn't really like you to take nature into your own hands. I had my mind on weeping willows and crepe myrtle. I went ahead and bought fifteen azaleas while I was there, some gardening gloves, and some rubber shoes for working in the yard. Comet was on sale so I went ahead and got twenty cans. I bought a set of dishes (four place settings) because Kenneth had come and taken mine while I was in Clemmonsville; I guess Lydia didn't have any dishes. Then I thought that wouldn't be enough if I should have company, so I got two more sets so that I'd have twelve place settings. I figured if I was to have more than twelve people for dinner then I'd need not only a new dining-room set but also a new dining room. I didn't have any place mats that matched those dishes so I picked up some and some glasses that matched the blue border on my new plates and some stainless because I had always loved that pattern with the pistol handle on the knife.

They had everything in this Revco. I thought if I couldn't sleep at night I'd make an afghan, so I picked out some pretty yarn, and then I thought, well, if I was going to start making afghans at night, I could get ahead on my Christmas shopping, and so I'd make an afghan for my mama and one for Paula, who had been calling me on the phone non-stop to make sure I hadn't reported the stolen car, and one for Martha that I'd make a little bigger than normal, which made me think that I hadn't been to the Diet Center in so long I didn't even know my weight, so I went and found the digital scales and put one right on top of my seventy-nine skeins of yarn. I bought ten each of Candy Pink, Watermelon, Cocoa, Almond, Wine, Cinnamon, Lime, and only nine of the Cherry because the dye lot ran out. It made me hungry, so I got some dietetic bonbons. By the time I got to the checkout I had five carts full and when that young girl looked at me and handed me the tape that was over a yard long, I handed her Kenneth I. Barkley's MasterCard and said, "Charge it."

It was too hot to work in the yard, and I was too tired to crochet or unpack the car and felt kind of sick to my stomach. Thinking it was from the bonbon I ate on the way home, I went to the bathroom to get an Alka-Seltzer, but Kenneth had taken those too, so I just took two Valiums and went to bed.

"I feel like a yo-yo," I told the shrink when Paula suggested that I go. All of my clothes were way too big, so I had given them to Martha as an incentive for her to lose some weight and had ordered myself a whole new wardrobe from Neiman-Marcus on Kenneth I. Barkley's MasterCard number. That's why I had to wear my KISS THE COOK apron and my leotard and tights to the shrink's. "My clothes should be here any day now," I told him, and he smiled.

"No, I feel like a yo-yo, not a regular yo-yo either," I said. "I feel like one of those advanced yo-yos, the butterfly model, you know where the halves are turned facing outward and you can do all those tricks like 'walk the dog,' 'around the world,' and 'eat spaghetti.'" He laughed, just threw back his head and laughed, so tickled over "eat spaghetti"; laughing at the expense of another human being, laughing when he was going to charge me close to a hundred dollars for that visit that I was going to pay for with a check from my dual checkbook, which was what was left of Kenneth I. Barkley's account over at Carolina Trust. I had already taken most of the money out of that account and moved it over to State Employee's Credit Union. That man tried to be serious, but every time I opened my mouth, it seemed he laughed.

But I didn't care because I hadn't had so much fun since Kenneth and I ate a half-gallon of rocky-road ice cream in our room there in Sea Island, Georgia.

"Have you done anything unusual lately?" he asked. "You know, like going for long rides, spending lots of money?"

"No," I said and noticed that I had a run in my tights. After that, I couldn't think of a thing but runs and running. I wanted to train for the Boston Marathon. I knew I'd win if I entered.

*   *   *

Lydia was ten years younger than Kenneth, I had found that out during the six weeks when he fluctuated between snappy and choked up. That's what I knew of her, ten years younger than Kenneth and studying to be a barmaid, and that's why I rolled the trees in the yard of that pitiful-looking house she rented with eleven rolls of decorator toilet paper. My new clothes had come by then so I wore my black silk dress with the ruffled off-the-shoulder look. Lydia is thirteen years younger than me and, from what I could tell of her shadow in the window, about twenty pounds heavier. I was a twig by then. "I'd rather be an old man's darlin' than a young man's slave," my mama told me just before I got married, and I said, "You mind your own damn business." Lydia's mama had probably told her the same thing, and you can't trust a person who listens to her mama.

I stood there under a tree and hoisted roll after roll of the decorator toilet paper into the air and let it drape over branches. I wrapped it in and out of that wrought-iron rail along her steps and tied a great big bow. I was behind the shrubs, there where it was dark, when the front door opened and I heard her say, "I could have sworn I heard something," and then she said, "Just look at this mess!" She was turning to get Kenneth so I got on my stomach and slid along the edge of the house and hid by the corner. I got my dress covered with mud and pine straw, but I didn't really care because I liked the dress so much when I saw it there in the book that I ordered two. The porch light came on, and then she was out in that front yard with her hands on her hips and the ugliest head of hair I'd ever seen, red algae hair that looked like it hadn't been brushed in four years. "When is *she* going to leave us alone?" Lydia asked, and looked at Kenneth, who was standing there with what looked like a tequila sunrise in his hand. He looked terrible. "You've got to do something!" Lydia said, and started crying. "You better call your lawyer right now. She's already spent all your money."

"I'll call Sandra tomorrow," Kenneth said, and put his arm around Lydia, but she wasn't having any part of that. She twisted away and slapped his drink to the dirt.

"Call *her*?" Lydia screamed, and I wished I had my camera to catch her expression right when she was beginning to say "her"; that new camera of mine could catch anything. "What good is that going to do?"

"Maybe I can settle it all," he said. "I'm the one who left her. If it goes to court, she'll get everything."

"She already has," Lydia said, sat down in the yard, and blew her nose on some of that decorator toilet paper. "The house, the money. She has taken everything except the Mazda."

"I got the dishes," he said. "I got the TV and the stereo."

"I don't know why you didn't take your share when you had the chance," Lydia said. "I mean, you could've taken the microwave and the silver or something."

"It's going to be fine, honey," Kenneth said, and pulled her up from the dirt. "We've got each other."

"Yes," Lydia nodded, but I couldn't help but feel sorry for her, being about ten pounds too heavy for her own good. I waited until they were back inside before I finished the yard, and then walked over behind the fish market where I had parked the car. There wasn't much room in the car because I had six loads of laundry that I'd been meaning to take to the subdivision Laundromat to dry. Kenneth had bought me a washer but not a dryer, and I should have bought one myself but I hadn't; the clothes had mildewed something awful.

Not long after that all my friends at the Diet Center took my picture to use as an example of what not to let happen to yourself. They said I had gone overboard and needed to gain a little weight for my own health. I was too tired to argue with Martha, aside from the fact that she was five times bigger than me, and I just let her drive me to the hospital. I checked in as Lydia Barkley, and since I didn't know how Lydia's handwriting looked, I used my best Kenneth imitation. "Her name is Sandra," Martha told the woman, but nobody yelled at me. They just put me in a bed and gave me some dinner in my vein and knocked me out. As overweight as I had been, I had never eaten in my sleep. It was a first, and when I woke up, the shrink was there asking me what I was, on a scale of one to ten. "Oh, four," I told him. It seemed like I was there a long time. Paula came and did my nails and hair, and Martha came and confessed that she had eaten three boxes of chocolate-covered cherries over the last week. She brought me a fourth. She said that if she had a husband, she'd get a divorce, that's how desperate she was to lose some weight, but that she'd stop before she got as thin as me. I told her I'd rather eat a case of chocolate-covered cherries than go through it again.

My mama came, and she said, "I always knew this would happen." She shook her head like she couldn't stand to look at me. "A man whose business in life depends on others taking to the bottle is no kind of man to choose for a mate." I told her to mind her own damn business, and when she left, she took my box of chocolate-covered cherries and told me that sweets were not good for a person.

By the time I got out of the hospital, I was feeling much better. Kenneth stopped by for me to sign the divorce papers right before it was time for my dinner party. His timing had never been good. There I was in my black silk dress with the table set for twelve, the lasagna getting ready to be thawed and cooked in the microwave.

"Looks like you're having a party," he said, and stared at me with that same look he always had before he got choked up. I just nodded and filled my candy dish with almonds. "I'm sorry for all the trouble I caused you," he said. "I didn't know how sick you were." And I noticed he was taking me in from head to toe. "You sure look great now."

"Well, I'm feeling good, Kenneth," I told him and took the papers from his hand.

"I'm not with Lydia anymore," he said, but I focused instead on signing my name, my real name, in my own handwriting, which if it was analyzed would be the script of a fat person. Some things you just can't shake; part of me will always be a fat person and part of Kenneth will always be gutter slime. He had forgotten that when he *had* me he hadn't wanted me, and I had just about forgotten how much fun we'd had eating that half-gallon of ice cream in bed on our honeymoon.

"Well, send me a postcard," I told him when I opened the front door to see Martha coming down the walk in one of my old dresses that she was finally able to wear. And then came Paula and the man she kept in her bedroom, and my mama, who I had sternly instructed not to open her mouth if she couldn't be pleasant, my beautician, the manager of Revco, my shrink, who, after I had stopped seeing him on a professional basis, had called and asked me out to lunch. They were all in the living room, mingling and mixing drinks; I stood there with the curtains pulled back and watched Kenneth get in that Mazda that was in my name and drive down Marnier and take a left onto Seagrams. Summer was almost over, and I couldn't wait for the weather to turn cool so that I could stop working in the yard.

"I want to see you do 'eat spaghetti,' " my shrink, who by then had told me to call him Alan, said and pulled a butterfly yo-yo like I hadn't seen in years from his pocket. I did it; I did it just as well as if I were still in the seventh grade, and my mama hid her face in embarrassment while everybody else got a good laugh. Of course, I'm not one to overreact or to carry a situation on and on, and so when they begged for more tricks, I declined. I had plenty of salad on hand for my friends who were dieting so they wouldn't have seconds on lasagna, and while I was fixing the coffee, Alan came up behind me, grabbed my love handles, and said, "On a scale of one to ten, you're a two thousand and one." I laughed and patted his hand because I guess I was still focused on Kenneth and where was he going to stay, in a pup tent? Some things never change, and while everybody was getting ready to go and still chatting, I went to my bedroom and turned my alarm clock upside down, which would remind me when it went off the next day to return the title to Kenneth's name and to maybe write him a little check to help with that MasterCard bill.

I could tell that Alan wanted to linger, but so did my mama and so I had to make a choice. I told Alan it was getting a little late and that I hoped to see him real soon, *socially*, I stressed. He kissed me on the cheek and squeezed my hip in a way that made me get gooseflesh and also made me feel sorry for both Kenneth and Lydia all at the same time. "A divorce can do strange things to a person," Alan had told me on my last visit; the man knew his business. He was cute, too.

"It was a nice party, Sandra," my mama said after everybody left. "Maybe a little too much oregano in the lasagna. You're a tad too thin still, and I just wonder what that man who calls himself a psychiatrist has on his mind."

"Look before you leap," I told her, and gave her seventy-nine skeins of yarn in the most hideous colors that I no longer had room for in my closet. "A bird in the hand is worth two in the bush."

"That's no way to talk to your mother," she said. "It's not my fault that you were overweight your whole life. It's not my fault your husband left you for a redheaded bar tramp."

"Well, send me a postcard," I said and closed the door, letting out every bit of breath that I'd held inside my whole life. I washed those dishes in a flash, and when I got in my bed, I was feeling so sorry for Kenneth, who had no birds in his hand, and sorry for Mama, who would never use up all that yarn. I hurried through those thoughts because my eyelids were getting so heavy and I wanted my last thought of the night to be of Alan, first with the yo-yo and then grabbing my hipbone. When you think about it, if your hipbones have been hidden for years and years, it's a real pleasure to have someone find them, grab hold, and hang on. You can do okay in this world if you can just find something worth holding on to.

Man Watcher

What's my sign? *Slippery when wet.* Do I want to see your etchings? *No.* Have you seen me somewhere before? *Maybe, since I've been somewhere before.* What's my line? Well, I've got quite a few, all depends on what I'm trying (or not trying) to catch.

It's not so hard to pick up a man, matter of fact it's one of the easiest things I've ever done. A good man? Well, that's something entirely different. Believe you me, I know. My step-sister, Lorraine, is always saying *like I don't know where you're coming from.* Like if I say I've got a migraine headache, she says, *"Like I don't know where you're coming from. I* have the kind of migraine that *blinds* you. The doctor says I might have the very worst kind of migraine known to man. My migraines are so horrendous I've been invited to go to Duke University for them to study me." You get the picture. *Like I don't know.* Lorraine knows a lot about everything and she has experienced the world in a way nobody can come close to touching. Still, when it comes to sizing up men, I've got her beat. I sit back and size them up while she jumps in and winds up making a mess of her life. When she opens her mouth in that long horsey way of hers, I just say *like I don't know where you're coming from.*

I've thought of publishing a book about it all, all the different types of the species. You know it would sort of be like Audubon's bird book. I'd call it *Male Homo Sapiens: What You Need to Know to Identify Different Breeds.* Natural habitats, diet, mating rituals. I'd show everything from chic condos to jail cells; from raw bloody beef to couscous and sprouts; from a missionary position (showers following) to an oily tarp spread out behind a Dempsey Dumpster. I'd break it all down so even the inexperienced could gain something. Of course there are a few questions that I haven't quite worked out yet. Like, why is it considered *tough* for a man (usually a big-city macho type) to grab himself and utter nasty things (such as an invitation to be fellated) to another man? Is there something hidden there, like in those seek and find pictures? And why don't men have partitions between urinals? Is there a history of liking to watch or something? Does it all go back to the Greeks and Romans where a little homosexual activity was perfectly in order, like a good solid burp at the end of a meal? I'm still working on a lot of topics, as you can see, but quite a bit of my research is already mapped out.

You know, you got your real *fun* guys that you love to date but you wouldn't want to marry—they'd be addicted to something and out of work about the time you hatch the first kid. Then you got the kind who might do all right in a job and lead a relatively clean life, but they bore you to tears. (I'm talking the kind that gets into little closet organizers and everything zipped up in plastic.) And you've got the kind you ought to leave alone—period. (I'm talking worthless pigs and middle-aged crazed sleazos.) That's where Lorraine screwed up (on both accounts) and I've told her so on many occasions. Her husband, Tim, likes to drink beer and scrunch the cans on the side of his head. He likes to chew tobacco while drinking beer and talk about what him and the boys *done and seen* while *hunting up some good fat quail and some Bambi.* He wears army fatigues and drinks some more beer and talks about needing to get some sex (actually, he uses all the slang terms for a woman's anatomy). He drinks still more beer and talks about needing to take a leak.

"Well, just be sure you put it back," I said not long ago, and Lorraine and her mother (my evil step-mother) gave me a long dirty look. My name is Lucinda, after my real mother's mother (I go by Luci), but every now and then I refer to myself as Cinda and bare my size six-and-a-half foot just so they have to take a good look at themselves:

mean ugly step-mother and self-centered step-sister, both with big snowshoe-type feet.

"Take a leak. Put it back. That's a good one now," Tim said and shuffled through his magazines until he found one of his choosing for a little bathroom time, *Soldier of Fortune* or *American Killer*, something like that. Lorraine and Mama, Too—as she *used* to beg me to call her when Daddy was still alive—were still staring. They have accused me of turning my back on my family and our natural ways because I lived in Washington, D.C., for a year, where I worked as a secretary in some very dull and very official office where there were a lot of very dull and very official men. I was there when there were rumors that this senator who wanted to be president (there are LOADS of men who fit into this particular *Homo sapiens* profile) had a mistress. This fellow always wins the election with the help of people like my step–brother-in-law who believe that there should be a gun in every home and that school cafeterias should be eternally stocked with that delicious vegetable, the catsup. What I still don't understand is who in the hell would go with that type? I'm an expert on these things and oftentimes am led by curiosity, but I have my standards. I mean, if you were the *wife* at least you'd live in a nice house in Georgetown or Alexandria, the fella wouldn't utter a peep if you dropped a few thou. But just to *go* with him, good God. Lorraine's friend, Ruth Sawyer, has dated a man for fifteen years with nothing to show for it. Stupid, I say.

I left D.C. (which was fine with me) when Daddy got so sick. I was allergic to those cherry trees the whole country raves about in the spring. Still though, if I ever even refer to the Smithsonian, Lorraine and Mama, Too roll their eyes and smirk at each other.

"You'd be lucky to get a man like Tim," my step-mother had said.

"Like I don't know," I told her. "There are very few men in his category."

"That's right." Lorraine nodded her head as she flipped through her husband's pile of arsenal magazines to find one of her beauty ones. Tim's breed happen to travel in camouflage clothes, but they like their women to sport loud and gaudy feathers and makeup. Of course she had enough sense to know that I was not being serious, so she turned quickly, eyes narrowing. "What do you mean, his category?"

"Not many men who read about the defense of the great white race while taking a leak," I said.

"Har de har har," Lorraine said. She has not changed a bit since they came into our lives not long after my mother died of liver disease. Mama, Too worked in the office of the funeral parlor, which was convenient. I called her a "widower watcher" then, and I still do. My daddy was not such a great man, but even he was too good for Mama, Too.

Before Lorraine met Tim, she dated the man who I file in the middle-aged crazed sleazo slot. You know the type, someone who is into *hair* (especially chest) any way he can get it: rugs, Minoxidil, transplants. That poor grotesquerie would've had some grafted on his chest if he could've afforded the procedure. He'd have loved enough hair on his head to perm and chest hair long enough to preen. You know the type of man I mean, the type that hangs out in the Holiday Inn lounge like a vulture, sucking on some alcoholic drink, his old wrinkled eyes getting red and slitty as he watches young meat file through the doorway. He likes chains and medallions and doesn't believe in shirt buttons.

"You're some kind of bad off, aren't you, Lorraine?" I asked one night after her MAN left, his body clad in enough polyester to start a fire that would rival that of a rubber tire company. "I bet he couldn't get it up with a crane." My daddy was dying of lung cancer even as I was speaking, though we hadn't gotten him diagnosed yet, and he let out with a laugh that set off a series of coughs that could have brought the house down.

"Don't you have any respect?" Mama, Too asked, and I turned on her. I said, "Look, I am over thirty years old and my step-sister there is pushing forty. It isn't like he can send me to my room and keep me from going to the prom. Besides," I added and pointed to him, "he wasn't respecting me when he and Mama were out cutting up all over town, pickling their livers and getting emphysema while I was babysitting every night of the week to pay for my own week at Girl Scout camp, which I ended up hating with a passion anyway because it was run just like a military unit."

What I didn't tell her, though, (what I've never told anyone) is that going to Girl Scout camp gave me my first taste of self-sufficiency. It had *nothing* to do with the actual camp, but was in my getting ready for it. I found stability in my little toiletries case: my own little personal bottles of shampoo and lotion. *My* toothbrush and *my* toothpaste. These smallest personal items represent independence, a sensation you need forever. Otherwise, you're sunk. I liked having everything in miniature, rationed and hidden in my bag. For that week (the only way I made it through their bells and schedules) I was able to pull myself inward, to turn and flip until I was as compact as one of those little plastic rain bonnets. It was the key to survival, and it had nothing to do with the woods (though I'll admit the birds were nice) or building a fire (I had a lighter). It had nothing to do with what leaves you could eat (I had enough Slim Jims along to eat three a day). It was my spirit that I had found. Of course I lost it the very next week once I was back home and doing as I pleased when I pleased, but I couldn't forget the freedom, the power my little sack of *essentials* had brought me.

"You could have benefitted from the military," Mama, Too said after I'd run down my career in the Girl Scouts. She was ready to spout on about her late great husband Hoover Mills and his shining military career. I told her his name sounded like an underwear or vacuum cleaner company.

"I have said it before," I told her, "and I'll say it again. I would never have a man of the church, and I would never have a man of the military. I don't want anybody telling me what to do or inspecting me." I emphasized this and looked at Mama, Too.

"Who's to say they'd have *you*?" Lorraine said.

"I could have that old piece of crap who just left here if I wanted him," I told her, and my daddy erupted in another phlegm fair, coughing and spewing and laughing.

"We are in love," Lorraine informed me, and to this day I remind her of saying that. I remind her when Tim is standing close by so I can watch her writhe in anger. I remind her whenever we ride by the Holiday Inn. I'll say, "Here to my left is the Holiday Inn, natural habitat of Lorraine's former lover, the middle-aged crazed sleazo of the Cootie phylum, complete with synthetic nest and transplanted feathers." Now whenever I say anything about Tim, the Soldier of UNfortune, she responds that same way: "I love him." I miss not having my daddy there to choke out some good belly laughs. Those attacks always bought me enough time for my comeback.

"It's easy to fall in love," I always say, "easy as rolling off a log, or if I were Mama, Too's boyfriend (a new one, just that fast!), easy as rolling off a hog."

"I know your soul is in the devil's hand," Lorraine says. "You wouldn't know love if it bit you."

"Oh, yes I would and, oh, yes it has," I say. "It's easy to

fall in love. What's hard is *living* with it. And if you can't live with it, you're better off without it." I wanted to add that Mama, Too had done a fine job killing off love but I let it ride.

I've never gotten into all that love/hate rigamarole like some women do. If I want lots of drama, I'll turn on my TV set. Any time of day you can turn on the tube and hear women talking about things they need to keep to themselves. I hear it when I go to the spa. There we'll be, bitching about cellulite and sweating it out in a sauna, and somebody will start. She'll talk about how her eye has been wandering of late, how her husband bores her, how he just doesn't turn her on, nothing, zippo. "What do you do for a wandering eye?"

"See the ophthalmologist?" I ask. "Go down to the livery stable and get yourself some blinders?"

"Oh, be serious, Luci," they say. "You DO like men, don't you?" It's amazing how whevever a woman is asked this question, other women get real uncomfortable while waiting for the answer. They check to make sure that no private parts are exposed for the wandering eye of a lesbian, which I am not. Still, I let them sweat it.

"I like men the same way I like people in general," I say. "Some I do and some I don't."

"You know what we mean," they say, and they all lean forward, more skin than swimsuits showing in this hot cedar box.

It's like a gigglefest in that sauna anytime you go. Something about the heat makes everybody start talking sex and fantasy. I tell them that they need some hobbies, get a needlepoint kit, bake a loaf of bread. The truth of it all is that I'm ahead of my time. I have already figured out what I need to live a happy healthy life and I'm no longer out there on the prowl. If my life takes a swing and I meet Mr. Right and settle into a life of prosperity then so be it, and if I don't then so be it. I'm in lover's purgatory. I've seen hell and I'm content to sit here in all my glorious neutrality.

One woman who was all spread out in a tight chartreuse suit said that she had a stranger fantasy. She said (in front of seven of us) that she thought about meeting a man in a dark alley and just going at it, not a word spoken. Well, after she told that not a word was spoken for several minutes, and then I got to feeling kind of mad about it all and I said that I just didn't think she ought to go touching a penis without knowing where it had been. "For health reasons," I added, but by then there were six near-naked women mopping up the floor with laughter and that seventh woman (Ms. Stranger in Chartreuse) shaking her head back and forth like *I* was stupid.

I was desperately seeking once upon a time. I was unhappily married to a man who wanted me to be somebody I wasn't and was forever making suggestions, like that I get my ears pinned, that I gain some weight, that I frost my hair, learn to speak Spanish, get a job that paid better, pluck off all my eyebrows, let the hair on my legs grow, and take up the piano so that I could play in the background while he read the paper. Now where was my little sack of security then? I was buying the jumbo sizes of Suave shampoo so I could afford the frostings and the Spanish tapes and the row machine. My essentials were too big to hide from the world. I once knew a girl who went to lunch from her secretarial job and never came back. I knew another girl who woke up on her wedding day with bad vibes and just hopped a jet and left her parents with a big church wedding mess. I admired them both tremendously. I once told Lorraine she should take lessons from such a woman, and she and Mama, Too did their usual eye rolling. It wouldn't surprise me if one day their eyeballs just roll on out like I've heard those of a Pekingese will do if you slap it hard on the back of the head.

Before I was married, I was a rock singer. I named my band The Psychedelic Psyches, you know after the chick Cupid liked. I saw us as soulful musicians, acting out some of our better songs with interpretive dance numbers. My parents called us The Psychedelic Psychos, which I did not appreciate. There were four of us in the band: I sang and played the drums; Lynn West, a tall thin brooding poet type, played the uke; Grace Williams, who was known for her peppy personality, could rip an accordian to shreds;

my friend Margaret played the xylophone and had a col-
lection of cowbells she could do wonderful things with.
We were just warming up on a local level when some jeal-
ous nothing type of a girl (someone like Lorraine) started
calling us The Psychedelic Sapphos and spreading rumors
about what we did in my GM Pacer, which we called "the
band wagon."

   "Oh, ignore it," I told them but Lynn and Grace quit.
They said they just couldn't have a connection like that,
not when Lynn was pre-engaged to a boy at Vanderbilt
and Grace was supposed to inherit her family's pickle business in Mt. Olive, North Carolina. "Good Lord," I said and
flipped my hair. It was as long as Cher's, and I was just as
skinny, if not more so. "It's a new generation." But their
response told me that men and pickles came first. Drugs
came first for Margaret, and we tried singing a few times
just the two of us, but she'd get really strung out and just go
wild with a cowbell. Margaret referred to our singing en-
gagements as *gigs*. All she talked about was gigs, gigs, gigs.
She'd call me on the phone in the middle of the night to ask
about a gig. Nobody wanted us and I knew that. The only
real *gig* we'd ever had anyway was doing little spontaneous
standups in a coffee shop downtown. Nobody wanted to
hear "Blowing in the Wind" sung to a cowbell from India.
Margaret liked to pass her time by doing LSD, and I passed
mine by searching for the perfect male, dissecting specimen
after specimen only to find his weaknesses and toss him

aside. I thought of myself as the female version of Dion's "The Wanderer." Or maybe I was "The Traveling Woman." It was wanderlust and lustwander; it got even worse after my mother died and my dad took up with Mama, Too.

I was taking pictures of being naked in a bed long before John and Yoko, *imagine* ha ha. I met my husband at a Halloween party and married him the next week. He looked much better when his face was painted up like a martian, and I guess I kept convincing myself that there would come a night when he would look that way again. My husband believed in unemployment and a working wife and all those other things I've mentioned. Lorraine said that I should've made my marriage work, should have gone into therapy instead of running off to D.C. I've told Lorraine that I could've kept that husband, could've made a go of that life-style. All I had to do was become a drug addict and hallucinate that everything was hunky-dory. I probably would've wound up like my friend Margaret, getting so high you'd have to scrape her off the ceiling. Finally she got scraped off a sidewalk. I was there when it happened. She said she was so high the only way down was to jump, and I was too busy talking to this matty-haired man to notice she meant business. He was wearing some of those suede German sandals that make people's feet look so wide; you know the kind, they're real expensive but they make you look like you don't have a pot to pee in and couldn't care less about your appearance. I had just asked him what made him buy those shoes, what image was he trying to fit (even then I was researching), when all of a sudden there were screams and people running to the window, the fire escape. There were sirens, a woman thinking she could fly like Peter Pan. You've heard it before. That man with the matted hair expected me to go home with him afterwards. Not long after that happened I met my future husband and decided to get married. I was convinced that I had snapped to, but my snapping to was like a dream inside of a dream, a hallway of doors where with every slam I woke up all over again. I had barely begun to snap to.

That night while staring down to where Margaret was under a sheet with a little cowbell clutched in her hand, the matty-haired fellow breathing down my neck, I knew there was something powerful I needed to commit to memory but all I was coming up with was things like *lay off the stuff*, *don't play on fire escapes*, *don't let yourself become so lonely*. But like a lot of people (like Lorraine) I translated that last one as needing somebody, which leads me back to what I've already told, a marriage made in hell and me now in lover's limbo. What I know now when I think of Margaret there, is that if you can't make it in life all by yourself (and by that I mean without benefit of people and substances and gigs of whatever sort you might crave), then you simply can't make it. That's the whole ball of wax. If it happens that you meet a person who walks right in and doesn't change a hair on your head, then your pie is *à la mode*. I've found in my research that this type of male is most often the kind you can't squeeze into a category. His lines are blurred and intertwined. He's a little bit of a lot of things, and a lot of what counts. His feathers are like none you've ever seen.

I'll hold out till I drop dead if I have to, and all the while I'm holding out I'll pursue my projects, my crafts, my academic studies on why some women go the route they do. Why does someone like Lorraine, who could educate herself and do better, settle; and why can't Mama, Too, who has already killed off two men (that I know of), give it up and take up cross-stitch? To think that a man can fill up whatever space you have is just stupid if you ask me. He can't do it any better than a box of Twinkies or a gallon of liquor, and to ask it of him is unfair.

So what's my line? What's my response? These days I'm not really playing. These days I'm constructing a little diorama of my apartment kitchen and in it I have a little clay figure who looks just like me and is working on a diorama of her apartment kitchen. I have always loved the concept of infinity; it makes me feel good. There is something about the large and small of the world, the connections and movement between the two that keeps me in balance. And if ever I need to feel even better about my life, I take *The Sound of Music* test, which assures me that my emotions are in working order. I have never once heard the Mother Superior sing "Climb Ev'ry Mountain" or watched the Von Trapps fleeing through the mountains at the end without getting a lump in my throat. It is a testament to life, to survival. I could watch that movie again and again. When we all rented it not too long ago, Lorraine said that the nuns depressed her. I assured her that the feeling would be mutual if the nuns ever met her.

And speaking of religious orders, right now I'm having a nice big argument with Mama, Too over what the rules for priesthood ought to be. I say (just to see what *she* will say) that celibacy means *no* sexual interaction at all, which includes people of the same sex as well as with yourself and by yourself. "Well, how do you propose that?" she asked. "You gonna wire them up so if they touch themselves it'll set off bells?"

"No," I tell her. "A solemn vow to God is good enough for me."

"What do you know of God?" she asks, and I'm about to tell her when her date walks in with a fifth of bourbon and a big slab of raw bloody beef.

"Why, Marty," I say to this old saggy cowboy. "I never noticed how hairy you are." He grins great big and hunkers down at the kitchen table. It's sad how easily some birds are bagged. He has molted down to a patchy-skinned bone. Mama, Too will have him henpecked in no time.

I guess in a way I'm waiting for the rarest breed of all, my sights set so high I have to squint to keep the sky in focus. I concentrate on migration habits. I keep in mind that owls fly silently at night. Some people (like Lorraine) might say I'm on a snipe hunt. But, call me an optimist. I'm sitting here in a pile of ashes, waiting for the phoenix to take shape and rise.

Gold Mine

The day the interstate opened was the day High-way 301 and Petrie, South Carolina, died. It used to be a hot spot, buzzing with a steady stream of cars heading to Florida. Ruthie Kates remembers it well, the whoosh of traffic, a rise and fall like the ocean waves that beckoned the tourists southward. That's how it was when she and Jim took over the Goodnight Inn and that's how it stayed for years. Then with the opening of I-95 the traffic veered inland and the flow slowed to a dribble, leaving behind a ghost town of pastel-painted motor lodges.

Just three weeks ago Jim veered off as well and the empty silence of the blazing afternoon has left Ruthie with nothing to do but sit by the pool and conjure the way it used to be. Her daughter Frieda is in the shallow end with a friend she met in Tiny Tots; already their eyes are red from the chlorine and their fingertips shriveled like raisins while they pretend to be mermaids with long flowing hair (both have the standard four-year-old pixie cut for summer). Rodney has twice ordered them out of the pool while he used the long net to fish out fallen leaves and then a tiny tree frog, which sent them screaming to the foot of Ruthie's chair. Rodney, who is nine, has asked very few questions since Ruthie explained that his father needed some time away, though at least once a day he pulls the phone into the bathroom and then whispers for what seems an eternity. "Who was that?" she has asked, only to be answered by a shrug. She knows he calls Malcolm, a boy in his class who is on his third father. Ruthie feels his stare often and tries to read his eyes; sometimes there is a look of pity and sometimes there is a look of anger. He knows more than he should, thanks to Malcolm. Now he is sailing pebbles across Highway 301 and into the deserted parking lot of the Budget Motel; his goal is to hit the NO TRESPASSING sign blocking the drive.

There was a time when the Budget Motel was always filled by late afternoon and then the Goodnight Inn caught the overflow. Ruthie and Jim would stand in the office and look out the big glass window, watching as car after car circled the Budget Motel's lot, crossed the road, and then turned into theirs; they would whisper ecstatic cheers, day after day, as they nonchalantly leaned outside to greet their guests. In only a few hours they would walk out together to hang the NO VACANCY sign, and Jim, energized by each passing day, would tell her that they were sitting on a gold mine. It was like his uncle Ross had said when he turned it over to them, a gold mine. They had plans, too. They would add on; build a couple of rooms on each end of the building; build a little recreation hall out back in the empty lot where the guests could play Ping-Pong; build their own house, the very house she wanted, hidden from the motel by a grove of trees.

Now when Ruthie remembers walking out to hang the sign with Jim, it's always sunset and there's always a breeze, a breeze that smells of citrus fruit and Coppertone lotion. It's always one of those days when her hair falls smooth as silk, glistening with gold highlights that show off her tan; and her legs are long and lean, graceful with every step, her stomach flat as she stands with her hands on her hips, white gauzy dress swirling around her. And in this memory Jim is always beside her, both arms wrapped around her waist as he nuzzles into her, the collar of his workshirt smooth against her cheek, his eyes a brilliant blue as he stares at that sign. That's the way she pictures it all, though she has never in her life owned a white gauzy dress and though, somewhere along the way, she was pregnant twice, and she knows that any good weather-record will show the intense humidity and breezeless days, the

rainy ones where they argued over who would suit up and
dash out there with an umbrella to hang the sign. They had
marveled at the Budget Motel; its VACANCY/NO VACANCY
sign was electric, instant neon thrown with a switch from
the warm dry attendant there in the lobby. "We'll have a
sign like that before long," Jim always said.

Ruthie and Jim got married right out of high school. His
uncle Ross was their only supporter, proof being his gift
of the motel. He said he was ready to get out of the business, ready to buy a condo in a retirement community.
The motel was in such a state of decay (Uncle Ross had
said it *could* be a gold mine) that they spent the first year
of marriage in a camper Ruthie's dad had bought a week
before he died. He had bought the camper with plans to
travel around the country with Ruthie's mother and see
what they had missed. For over a year it had sat, flat and
compact, in the back drive, while her mother periodically
made mention of the money she *would* have had if not for
the camper. Ruthie's offer to buy it was the beginning of her
mother's acceptance of the marriage. Jim came and pulled
the camper home and then it was as simple as flipping out
the sides like wings (each formed a double bed). A canvas
roof arched above. It had a tiny refrigerator and zippered
windows.

"For godssakes," Jim's mother had said, "isn't it bad
enough without you two living in a tent?"

They were in the camper all those late nights when they huddled together and made plans for the future. They would turn the motel around and then sell it for a great profit. They would move to Columbia, where both of them would go to college. He would be an architect and she would be an interior designer. They might have their own business, a team to go in and refurbish old buildings and homes. But in the meantime they had gotten a loan and were slowly redoing the Goodnight Inn, painting and cleaning. Ruthie put every bit of time and energy into the motel. They spent one week in old bathing suits, scrubbing out the drained pool, and then repainting the plaster a deep cool aqua. Their bodies speckled with paint, they had stretched out on the concrete and talked about their accomplishments, when they would open, how soon they could begin filling the pool. "It's a gold mine," he said, his large tanned hand cupping hers as they lay there staring up at the sky and listening to the steady flow of cars in and out of the Budget Motel.

It was her idea to paint the building pink, to make it look tropical so people heading to Florida would be put in the mood sooner. By the time they reopened, she was three months pregnant with Rodney, and the business prospect was booming. If they had had a hundred rooms they could have filled them.

Ruthie's mother, now fully accepting and approving, helped out with the cleaning while Ruthie began the *real* decorating, the colors and textures and framed prints that would replace the drab tan walls and white chenille spreads and wall calendars that Jim's uncle had received in bulk from the local Chevrolet dealer (each month showed off a different car model).

Ruthie took great pride in the fact that no two rooms were the same; each had its own theme, its own mood, and she secretly named them as she sat at the sewing machine, her kitchen chair pushed back from the table as her abdomen grew round and hard. Jim said he saw no reason to go to all that trouble and expense when the rooms were renting just fine as they were. But she saw it as a challenge, the power to create a mood, colors changing in the same way the mood ring Jim had given her responded to her change in body temperature. She felt so hot during her pregnancy that she had called room number one "Tahitian Treat," decorating it with cool shades of pink and green, a tropical spread on the bed, a seashell print on the wall. She had then done what she called "Sunshine Saffron" and "Forest Foliage" and "Lavender Lace."

She had just finished number six, "Blue Moon," when Rodney was born, and sometimes around midday when there *were* vacancies, this is where she went with him. The air-conditioning unit rumbled there under the window, all heat and bright summer sun blocked out by the navy curtains, as she stretched her legs out on the shimmering chintz spread and stared up at the print she had hung of a big crescent moon over the sea. One day Jim eased open the door, a harsh blast of light and heat, and then came and stretched out beside her. Within minutes, his head was pressed against the crook of her arm and he, like Rodney, was sound asleep.

This is another memory she thinks about these days as she watches the empty highway—the wonderful sensation of that cool dark room. Now Rodney is determined to hit the sign across the street; he has traded his pebbles for hard clumps of clay and is hurling them faster and faster. His jaw is clenched, his face red, as he exhales and lunges forward with each throw. He finally hits and the sign creaks back and forth on its chain.

Rodney was four when Frieda was born. By then they had built the house back behind the motel, a white two-story house with a wraparound porch. The recreation facility had a huge stone fireplace, two Ping-Pong tables and a shuffleboard court. They added an efficiency on the far end of the building, a special honeymoon suite with a huge bathtub up on a platform. The room curved out towards the highway and had exposure on all four sides. From the window over the queen-size waterbed, you could see their house, hanging begonias swinging on the porch, and from the bathroom, you could see the office, new glass windows and fluorescent tubing that glowed all night.

Some nights Ruthie's mother came to baby-sit, and they drove off like they were going into town to the movies and then circled back and parked at the end of the lot where it was dark. They would sneak into number fifteen, where they turned on the radio and danced naked up the platform and into the huge tub. If they didn't turn on any lights they could lift one shade and see the moon, the palmettos in the yard, headlights circling the ceiling as they lay there in the warm water. Some nights they lay there until the water got cool and then, the air-conditioning unit turned on high, they ran to the bed and climbed under the wine-colored satin comforter Ruthie had driven to Columbia to buy. Jim set his tiny travel alarm for eleven o'clock, and they bolted with the sound, shocked to find themselves removed from their normal place. They whispered and laughed while dressing to drive the fifty yards home as if they were still in high school and sneaking in from a date. Part of the fun was that it *was* a secret, that they could hold hands, squeezing to suppress laughter when her mother said things like, "Big crowd to see Sean Connery, I reckon."

Now, with the exception of an occasional clump of clay hitting the Budget's NO TRESPASSING sign, there is silence, a wide flat silence, while over there on I-95 the traffic flows, heavy and steady. Now the VACANCY sign has rusted in place, the letters faded to a fleshy pink. Ruthie sits by the pool; behind her chair in rooms ten and eleven, "Magic Carpet Ride" and "Spring Meadow," the venetian-glass doors seal in darkness.

Jim has been gone for the longest three weeks of her life, and 301 is without a doubt dead, no resurrection in sight. Frieda and her friend are doing what they call bump bottoms; they hold hands, press the soles of their feet together, and pull back such that they go under water and their bottoms collide. "Bump bottoms!" they scream when they rocket to the surface in laughter; they can do this for hours and Ruthie will probably let them until the sun sets and it's time to go inside and go to bed.

The sun is finally low in the sky (daylight saving time does not make life any easier), and soon she can call the kids inside to dinner and then gather in front of the television for yet another night of sitcoms. While they watch, she can slowly ease herself into her gown and then into her bed, where she can finally give into the growing desire to close her eyes and sleep through it all. It is like he robbed her energy supply and crammed it into the suitcase with all of his underwear.

An occasional car passes on the highway, usually a local going to or from the shopping center. Sometimes it's her mother, who says she just happened to be passing by, which is an overt lie; these *happenings* never occurred three weeks before, but Ruthie bites her tongue. Why should she blame her mother for asking all of the same questions she's asking herself? It's hard *not* to ask how she got here. How Rodney grew so fast from that warm little body she cuddled there in the Blue Moon Room. How Frieda went from being a plump little baby who refused to walk until she was fif-

teen months old to this long-legged colt. Jim had called
Frieda "Buddha" when she sat round and placid in the center of the room and pointed to what she wanted, grunted a
command. In the mornings when the teakettle whistled,
Frieda shrieked after it, a high wailing *Wooooooooooooo*
which sent Rodney into a fit of laughter; it sent *all* of them
into a fit of laughter. So how had it happened?

How can you be laughing one day and crying the next,
and how had the years taken such a sudden turn? How had
301 died such a quick tragic death, and when had Jim ever
had the time to meet someone else, and not just to meet
her but to court her, to woo her, to sleep with her right
there in number fifteen while just twenty yards away she
had sat under the fluorescent light of the office and waited
for the check-in that never came, waited for the phone call
that would reserve the entire motel? These were the stories
she was telling him, and he was telling her, these stories
about how people would get tired of the sameness of the
interstate, tired of those SOUTH OF THE BORDER and MYRTLE
BEACH signs, how the people would come back. Why, any
day now, old 301 would be buzzing. And in the midst of
all of this futile optimism, she had been completely blind
to what was happening. She had fallen for the very trick
that she and Jim had used on her mother; he was in room
fifteen, right there under her nose.

"Watch this," Frieda calls now and does a cannonball,
arms hugging her knees as she slaps into the water and

sprays her pale giggling friend who clings to the ladder. Ruthie wishes that Rodney and Frieda *would* ask her some questions. What happened? Will he come back? Is it your fault that he left? Instead, she has heard them whispering back and forth and she tries not to think of what Rodney, in the vocabulary of Malcolm, is telling Frieda. *They will get a divorce. We will never see him again. He doesn't love us anymore. He wanted to sell the motel and go to school years ago but she talked him into staying.*

Ruthie keeps thinking she needs some advice, an opinion, but is afraid to seek it because everyone in town will hear the news as fast as she opens her mouth and there will be desperately lonely people knocking on her door; nothing like a good bit of domestic dirt to shake up a ghost town or to lend hope to the other singles in need. Once she and Jim had spent a whole Friday evening sitting by the pool with a psychiatrist and his wife who were on their way to see the man's family in Miami. Ruthie had been afraid to talk at first. Neither the man's voice nor his wife's carried a trace of an accent, but it was more that she was afraid he would read something in her every word. Finally, after everyone except her had had a couple of glasses of wine and an hour of idle conversation about the difference between a palmetto and a palm, she got used to the fact that he was as normal as Jim. She was six months pregnant with Frieda at the time and had Rodney clinging to her legs. She had asked the doctor lots of questions about bringing in a new baby, how to make it all easy on Rodney, while the doctor's wife and Jim talked about astronomy, pointing out this or that constellation or planet. After another hour of chatting, Jim had gone in and gotten an old telescope that he hadn't used in years, and the two of them sat there searching the sky. He had talked about college, what he planned to take when he finally got there. Maybe Jim had always been looking. That's what Ruthie should have asked the psychiatrist. What are the signs of a husband about to leave?

"Did you see me, Mom?" Frieda calls, thumbing the back of her bathing suit where it rode up with the impact of her landing. Ruthie nods and then waves to Mrs. Andler, who is sitting outside of the Blue Moon room in another of the worn-out lawn chairs. Mrs. Andler moved in when she decided at eighty that her house in town was much too large for her. Ruthie gave her a good deal when she moved in a month ago and has yet to have the nerve to approach her about whether she sees this as a temporary or permanent thing. "You can't start this, Ruthie," Jim said just two days before he left. "We are not running a rest home. Uncle Ross *left* here to *go* to a retirement area, remember?" *We*, he said *we* are not running a rest home.

"We're not running anything right now," she had said. "We haven't rented a room in over three weeks." And she had reluctantly allowed Mrs. Andler to pick her own room, knowing that there was a good chance that she'd pick the coolest, the darkest, her own personal favorite. Still, it was steady rent and Ruthie didn't see what *would* be so terrible about having a few senior citizens around the place. So put up a few toilet bars, widen a doorway. What's in Florida anyway?

"You're not listening," he said, the muscle in his jaw tight. "You're not even trying to see."

Now she thinks he meant more than that. Maybe he wanted her to *see*. Just a week before, he had teased her about a boy who had been in their high-school class, a boy who always sent a Christmas card and stopped by to say hello if he was passing through. "There's a catch, Walter the Weird," Jim said. "Eight feet tall and a hundred and twenty pounds."

"Oh, well," she said and laughed. "And I suppose you've got some real looker after you." And she teased him about a girl in the class a year ahead of them. "What about you and Loose Linda?" she asked. "What about that purple sequin dress she wore to the prom? Clashed with her orange hair something awful." Now Linda runs a local jewelry store and has fingernails long enough to rival those of Howard Hughes. She reminded him of that, too, all the while seeing a picture in her mind of the prom their junior year: Jim on the dance floor with Linda, her standing in front of the refreshments with smart Walter. Walter was talking about how he wanted to have a single room at the University so that he wouldn't have to make compromises about his study time, and Ruthie was thinking about how she'd like to march out on the dance floor and grab Linda by the throat.

"At least Walter is a CPA. I hear he buys his wife something extravagant every single April. For all I know he buys it from Linda." There was a moment of silence and she read it as the same old sore spot, education, so she continued talking, something she had always done well. "Don't you remember that prom?" she asked. "You came over and asked me to dance while Linda went to the bathroom?"

"Yeah."

"You asked me out for the very next night, said it was dumb that we had broken up to begin with. You did all that right there under Linda's long nose." She thought they had *both* gotten a good laugh, a playful exchange that led to a kiss and a hug, a long hard hug, his day-old beard rubbing her cheek. Now she thinks he pulled her close so she couldn't see his eyes, couldn't see the dishonesty. Now she thinks that he was trying to prepare her, trying to make her think about herself and what kind of man she would attract, make her stop and ask herself if she was still attractive.

"I saw *you*." That's what she had said that night when Jim tried to offer an explanation. The ends of his hair were still wet from the tub; for all she knew the woman (he had called her Barbara) was still down there in number fifteen, a damp naked body stretched out on the sheets Ruthie had changed that very morning.

Ruthie, drawn in some strange way—maybe by a thought of those wonderful nights they had spent in the Honeymoon Tub—had stepped from the office into the empty parking lot. It was unseasonably pleasant for a night in July and she had turned slowly into the breeze, the Budget Motel across the highway already dark and boarded up, the lights in her own house glowing where her mother sat reading to the kids. The window to their bedroom was open, and she could see the sheers blown to one side, showing a perfect rectangle of darkness. She imagined Jim sitting in a school desk, his long legs stretched on a linoleum floor while he listened to someone lecturing on hotel management, Options During the Slow Season, a two-week course offered at the community college an hour south on 301.

The thought of him there, a tired knowing look on his face, had made her homesick for when they had just started, homesick for all those days they had walked out to the road to hang the NO VACANCY sign or even before, those late afternoons in the camper, his how-to books thrown on one bed while the two of them curled up on the other. She had liked the way his shirts looked hanging over the other bed, his guitar up where the pillow should be. *We'll show them*, they had said too many times to count; that's the

kind of promise she missed and needed. She had wanted
to stretch out on the bed in Blue Moon, only Mrs. Andler
had beaten her to it, and already she could hear the opening music to "Falcon Crest" coming through the Venetian-
glass door; Mrs. Andler had probably fallen asleep as she
did every night, the *sounds of the stories* keeping her from
having thoughts that would keep her awake.

So Ruthie tiptoed past Blue Moon and then ran past all
the other dark doors until she got to the end, the familiar
key on the ring already pressed in her palm, an involuntary
act. It slipped into the lock and she crept in, soothed by the
darkness for that half of a second before she heard a splash.
She froze, first expecting a thief, a stranger. "Barbara," he
said, and she could not move, her legs paralyzed. It was
after a series of sounds, slips and slides and groans, that
her voice came back to her, only it didn't sound like her
voice at all. "Jim!" she screamed. "Jim, is that you?" And
then within minutes, he stumbled out in front of her, a
towel around his waist, and there in the dark bathroom
before the door slammed shut, she saw the profile of a
woman sitting straight up, arms crossed, hands covering
her breasts.

Jim looked as handsome at that moment as he had ever
looked, and it made her sick that she even thought it. He
kept opening his mouth as if he had something to say (It's
not what you think. I have no idea how this happened.)
but realized that there was nothing he *could* say, absolutely

nothing, at least at that moment, and before he had time to think of something, she turned and ran, leaving the door to number fifteen standing open.

Her mother would have known with one glance that something had happened, and she was not up to facing her. She searched her pockets for the car keys but they were on top of her dresser, dropped as they were every night into the pink silk box that she had received when Frieda was born. At a loss, she went into the office and turned her stool towards the wall where hung the last of the auto calendars, a turquoise Chevette front and center. Below it in bold letters, MAY DAY.

Jim came in and stood behind her for a long time without saying a word. She could see in the reflection of the plastic-coated bulletin board that he kept reaching a hand out and then drawing it back. The reflection of his hand kept reaching right into a notice about AKC poodles, and then into one about a Jane Fonda aerobics course that took place each weeknight in the Petrie Junior High School Cafeteria. Jim said it had never happened before, a first, and though she didn't believe that, though she sensed *habit* and *pattern* in the whole fiasco, she said so what if it was the first, did that make it right?

When it was finally late enough that she knew her mother was asleep in the guest room, she went up to the house, Jim right behind her. She kept looking around for *Barbara*, kept wanting to ask how and when he met

Barbara, but the night was silent. He brushed his teeth and got in their bed as if they would sleep on it, talk it over in the morning over a strong pot of coffee and frozen waffles. She stayed up the entire night, checking on Rodney and Frieda every thirty minutes, needing to put her hand out and feel their warm breath. She could not shake the picture of the two bodies, there in her bathtub, in her number fifteen. It wasn't necessary to have a face for Barbara. Barbara had any and every face that he had ever stopped and noticed. Barbara had a perfect young lineless body, and she was brilliant and funny and talented in every way. Barbara told him that of course he should be in school, no woman in her right mind would deprive such a man. Ruthie finally slept on Frieda's bed, her face pressed into the hard plastic face of a baby doll, a hideous baldheaded baby whose name oddly enough was Barbara Jean.

Jim left the very next day. Ruthie woke with a stiff neck to see Frieda still asleep, mouth open and drooling onto Barbara Jean's nightgown. She woke with the slamming of a car door and looked out in time to see him leaving, Rodney standing in the middle of the parking lot, waving. "What is going on?" her mother asked and stepped into the room, a sealed envelope in her hand, Ruthie's name printed in his handwriting, a script as unruly as his and Rodney's hair. "Jim barely even spoke to me this morning. Didn't even eat his waffles and I thought he loved them."

*   *   *

He had met Barbara *at*, of all places, the community college, where she was an assistant instructor in some kind
of real estate or insurance. She was right out of college
and so he felt she was a good person to talk to about
courses and credits. He never meant for anything to happen. It all started with one little cup of coffee. But didn't
Ruthie *know* that something had been wrong? Couldn't she
tell that things weren't working? It wasn't just the ten-
sion of the highway going to pot, it was more. *Don't you
see, Ruthie, that it was more?* No, no she couldn't; she had
always thought things were getting *better*.

Ruthie hasn't gone after all the facts even though she is
certain her mother could supply them. What she has come
up with on her own is enough. Barbara is like I-95. She is
fast and lively and young, and Ruthie is 301, miles of tread
stains and no longer the place to go. She imagines Barbara
sidling up to Jim at school, her teeth clenched, jaw set in
that tense way that suggests sexual frustration, bitterness,
determination, or any combination of the three. She's seen
the look before, on dance floors, across the pool, window
to window on the highway, but she's never imagined Jim
on one side of it. She's never imagined that people would
be whispering *does his wife know?* and the wife would be
her. Now she can only suspect that there are people feeling
sorry for her; there are people who see her as a loser and,

thus, an easy catch. And this Barbara probably hates her with a passion, probably bristles with the sound of her name or the thought of her home even though they've never even been introduced.

"Bump bottoms!" Frieda sprays a mouthful of water, her hair sticking up all around her head in hundreds of cowlicks. Rodney is tossing a clay clod high into the air and counting the seconds before it drops. The sun is disappearing now, this very second, and before it does, Ruthie goes and switches on the pool lights, round circles of white light bringing cheers from the girls. When she squats to tell them that they can only swim ten more minutes, she breathes in the heavy chlorine, enjoying the odor as if it is bleaching every tiny hair in her nose, purifying her system.

"Good night now," Mrs. Andler calls and waves a rolled-up magazine. She holds on to the door facing as she slowly pulls herself into the room, the gray of her TV buzzing on to light the room before she closes the door.

The sun disappears behind the cracked billboard of the Budget Motel, leaving the empty pool out front dark like a crater. Watching the deserted building makes Ruthie's skin tingle, makes her shiver, even though it is still eighty-odd degrees. And then, after what seems like an eternity of silence, there are headlights coming down 301, familiar in shape and speed. Rodney has counted very fast to get to fifteen before his clay hits the concrete around the pool and shatters.

"Bump bottoms!" Frieda screams while the car turns in slowly, past the faded sign and into a space at the end of the lot. Ruthie concentrates on the pool, the water an odd shade of aqua green with the white lights shimmering beneath. It's the shade of green that makes her think of the 1940s, her own parents moving to the music of Glenn Miller. It makes her think of black-and-white tile floors and the sound of a saxophone. Frieda is standing in the shallow end wiping the water from her red eyes. Rodney has stopped throwing and is staring. She knows he's behind her now, and she watches Frieda's friend hold her nose and squat to the bottom. She focuses on the lights, round white lights like moons, like what she'd imagine on another planet, an empty barren planet. Maybe he's come home. Maybe this is it.

"Hey, kids," he says, and she jumps with his voice, not fully believing that he is really there. She turns and looks at him then, hands in the pockets of his jeans, hair neatly combed, face shaven, new knit shirt. Rodney has sidled up to him like a puppy and now is giving a play-by-play of every Little League game since his dad left home. Jim's hand is on his back. Frieda runs a circle around him, *Daddy, Daddy, Daddy,* and then jumps back in the pool. "Hi," he says, and Ruthie mouths the word back to him.

"Can we have another ten minutes?" Rodney asks, looking first at his dad. "Just ten?"

"Just ten." Ruthie stands. She stares in the pool as Frieda and her friend try to sit crosslegged on the bottom. Then

she takes a step towards him, watching her feet so as to
bypass the wet puddles and clumps of clay. *Have you come
home?* She imagines herself saying the words and is just
about to when she glances over at his car and sees a sil-
houette, a headful of curly curls. The sight makes her own
hand fly up to her head, the flat bangs, the back yanked
up with a silver barrette. There is no white gauzy dress
but a loose cotton shift, paint splattered and smelling of
chlorine.

"I thought you'd be up in the house," he says and steps
closer, seeing that she has seen, maybe knowing what it
was she was about to say. "Ruthie?" The sound of him
questioning her name makes her breathe quickly and when
she looks up he has stepped even closer, close enough
to touch. "Are you okay?" With every word out of his
mouth, she feels herself drawn closer. This is that old
feeling, that lean-against-the-locker-and-whisper-secrets-
about-the-rest-of-your-lives feeling, that surge of friendli-
ness and excitement that comes with the uncertain future,
the uncrossed threshold. She has an urge to hit him, to hug
him, and she knows her jaw is set in that same tight way
that she has seen and despised in other women. She knows
when she looks him in the eye that he is seeing all of this
in her and, whether he likes it or not, he is feeling something similar. He may not be thinking about hanging the NO
VACANCY sign or a night *they* spent in the honeymoon suite.
Maybe he never thinks about lying in that small camper

or about after the Labor Day picnic the beginning of their senior year when they snuck into the dark woods along the road and lay on a blanket, the large drive-in screen in the distance, Doris Day rushing around in silence. But he's got to be thinking and feeling something. He couldn't just *stop* thinking.

"So, did you give Mrs. Andler a contract?" He asks and stares into the pool where Frieda's friend is splashing her arms and legs in an attempt to turn a back flip.

"Yes." She feels brave and looks at him but his eyes are still on the pool. "I told her no loud music, no pets, and no men after midnight."

"Kind of strict."

"Based on a recent incident." She walks to the edge of the pool and is about to call the kids out, her heart pounding, head light and still ringing with the words she had not *planned* to say.

"I came to get some things," he says now, and again steps closer. "I had really thought you'd be up at the house at this time." Had he *hoped* that he'd find her in the house? To have her alone, out of Barbara's vision? To talk to her? To be with her? "You know, Frieda usually is getting ready for bed about now."

"Guess you can't always be too sure about what's *usually* going on." She glances over at the empty front seat of his car (had she imagined the woman?) and then turns back to him, eye to eye, and steps closer. She feels powerful all of a sudden, like she did years ago at that prom when she danced with him while long-nailed Linda was in the bathroom. This is how Barbara must have felt when she sauntered into number fifteen and stepped out of her clothes. Ruthie is close enough to put her hand on his, to wrap both hands around his throat and squeeze, to pull him close, but all thoughts are interrupted (haven't they always been interrupted?) by the splash of a cannonball, Rodney firing himself into the deep end, a wave of water cresting over the side.

She waits until the pool settles, feels his arm brush against hers as they stare over at the Budget Motel and the large NO TRESPASSING sign. "I need to go up to the house for a while," he whispers, and she feels the hair on her neck standing. "Go with me."

"Don't you have a date tonight?" she asks, her voice much weaker than she had intended. That's what she had asked him while they were on the dance floor, poor Walter keeping a vigil by the Kool-Aid–like punch, Linda in the doorway scanning the crowd.

He sighs and for a split second it looks as if he's going to reach for her hand, but he catches himself. No response. Rodney is counting now, a clod of dirt sailing upwards and then returning with a splat on the wet concrete. "You really should work on your style," she continues, gaining strength from every piece of dirt that flies. "A bird in the hand doesn't necessarily apply to people. Chances are you may find an empty nest."

"So maybe I will," he is saying, the back of his hand brushing hers. "Work on my style, I mean." It seems like an eternity that they stand there, his arm finding its way around her waist. She is thinking that it's too easy, that she needs to make things harder. It's always been so easy, as easy as forgetting about Walter, as easy as holding his hand and letting him pull her up and away from the lot of the drive-in where they spread a blanket over the damp pine straw. But hadn't she also pulled him, hadn't they pulled each other into a life that took shape so fast they hardly had time to think about it? Couldn't it just as easily have been her to fall into something? And if it hadn't been for her crazy rooms and their decorator colors, she probably would have noticed that something wasn't right. Her mind free of paint fumes and drapery patterns, and she might have fallen into something herself; she would have at least considered it, some smooth-talking white collar man to buy her something extravagant every April. They were young people leading an old life, complete with commode bars she had recently ordered for Mrs. Andler's room. But it's not over. She turns quickly and wraps her arms around him, as if on the dance floor or stretched out on the ground. She stares at the car, now certain that there never was anyone there. She thinks of Linda in her awful purple dress as she stood in the doorway of the gym, light from the hall illuminating her like some kind of out-of-date paper doll.

"God, what was I thinking?" he asks but she remains silent, lets her jaw relax. There will come a day when it will seem like it never happened, just as it sometimes surprises her to recall how the motel first looked, those bare dirty rooms. Somewhere along the way their vows to the justice of the peace, who was dressed in Bermuda shorts and a baseball jersey, have taken on the formal glow of a big church wedding, and their nights in the cramped camper have become hours of late-night talks and lovemaking and side-splitting laughter. And in a few years when they've sold the property and moved to Columbia, when Jim has graduated and Rodney writes to tell Malcolm that none of his predictions came true and Frieda is begging to wear makeup and stay out late, they will talk about the Goodnight Inn and how wonderful it was to live there, the traffic a steady flow of honeymooners and college kids and families in wood-paneled station wagons bound for the coast. They will almost forget these three lousy weeks. She listens to Rodney counting higher than he has all day, his pieces of dirt soaring into the sky, and she watches Frieda swim up to one of the round hazy lights, her small hand reaching for the moon.

First Union Blues

I'm sitting here at work knowing full well that the Mr. Coffee that my cousin Eleanore gave me for Christmas is going full blast and there's not a thing I can do about it. I knew as soon as I pulled into the parking lot that I forgot to turn it off. I knew when I looked up at our sign here in front of the bank that gives the time and temp; it said 80 F and I thought, hot, Jesus it is hot, blazing hot, and since I have a fear of fire and have my entire life since I saw the movie *Jane Eyre*, I happened to think of the Mr. Coffee and how I had thought I might want to drink that little bit there in the bottom after I put on my makeup and somehow in the midst of mascara and cover up, my mind wandered right on into wanting to wax my legs and see how it did. "It hurts like hell," Eleanore has said and that's what I was thinking right up until I parked and saw the time-and-temp sign.

I don't tell anybody this but I've yet to learn the C temp and how to figure it out and so I always have to wait around for the F one. What bothers me is that some days waiting for the time to flash up is like waiting for Christmas and other good days—before you can make it out (all the dots don't always work), it's all changed on you. That's how it was this morning. I don't know who here is in charge of that sign; I'm not. I'm a teller, which they tell me is "a foot in the door," "a base to grow upon," and so on. A check to pay off Visa is more like it.

There's nothing I can do about the Mr. Coffee right this second. I barely get a coffee break and I know they aren't going to let me drive clear across town to check on something that I might or might not have done. It's happened before that I have thought the oven was on and such, only to find that I had turned it off without even knowing. "I live by my instincts," I've told Eleanore and that's true. And so I could've cut it off, instinctively. All of us have done things instinctively only to find out we didn't remember doing it. Some people spend years that way.

Eighty-two degrees Farenheit. I can read it loud and clear, not a dot out of place, and I know that any minute now that condo I rent is going to bust into flames. It starts there at the Mr. Coffee, wedged right between the microwave and the wok: a little piece of paper towel ignites, catches hold of my new Dinah Shore kitchen rags, which are just for show and stay dry as a bone since my condo has a dishwasher and I let the dishes air dry. It spreads from there past the condo's miniblinds to my little oil lamp that says "Light My Fire" and that I won at a fair once for hitting a woman's big round butt with a beanbag. I never would've picked that lamp but free is free and so I took it and went ahead with Larrette over to the funny mirrors, which is all she wanted to do. "Fat," she would say and hide between my legs. She is only two and doesn't have many more words than what she saw in the mirrors—*big*, *little*, *funny*, and of course, *kitty* and *puppy*. There weren't any animals at the fair but those are her favorite words. If she likes something she'll call it kitty. If I could rig up some mirrors at home like that, she'd stay busy for hours but I'm not real sure how it's all done, which I guess is why you only see them at a fair or someplace special. I bought a little compact at Woolworth's that was on the sale table, and that mirror was so bad and wavy, I just knew Larrette would love it. She threw it to the floor and it cracked and sparkled all over the condo kitchen. "Seven years, puppy," I said to her but I'm not worried. I figure I've had my seven already.

Larrette is my daughter by Larry Cross of Shallotte, North Carolina, and he is—cross I mean. So we never see him at all, mainly because he lives in California doing odd jobs. "The sea is in my blood," he used to say just because he grew up in Shallotte, which is nothing but a spit from the ocean. And I told him that, yeah, if stretching out in the sun with little to no clothes on, sipping a Bud, and riding the waves is what it takes to have the sea in your blood, well then, yeah boy, I've got it in mine, too. "Only that kind of blood calls for money," I told him. "The average American cannot sunbathe straight from May to September." I meant due to finances, of course, but I couldn't even if I was Jackie O. because I'm fair-skinned; a strawberry blonde almost always is and my dermatologist tells me that skin cancer is bad in this area. That's probably one reason right there why I instinctively took up with Larry Cross. He had the tan that I had never had; he could have passed for Spanish if he could have kept his mouth shut which he couldn't. Open his mouth and Shallotte was written all over him.

I tell people that Larry Cross does odd jobs in California, when the truth is that I have no earthly idea what he does and I didn't when I was staying there with him in Fuquay-Varina. I think he must've dealt in drugs or something underhanded from the looks of the people who would appear at my door at all hours of the night and day when decent people are either at work or at home watching TV.

I never married Larry Cross because I wasn't about to saddle myself with trash. I say that now, but I guess there were some times when I thought we would get married; I guess I was thinking that when I was carrying Larrette and he was so proud of himself for getting me that way. And just as soon as Larrette had popped out Larry went and bought himself a surfboard with no surf whatsoever there in Fuquay-Varina (my instincts told me it wouldn't work). There were bills to pay which I had always paid and he was over there drinking a beer and listening to the Beach Boys singing, "Catch a wave and you're sitting on top of the world."

"What're you going to do come low tide?" I asked him. What we had wasn't a home, so one day I just up and left, me and Larrette. We moved to Raleigh and stayed with Eleanore until I got my job here. Then before I knew it, I was going to the state fair and living in a condo with a wreath on every wall and a big hooked rug that I bought at the outlet mall over near the airport. That place has got everything you might want and then some. Everything.

If that oil lamp catches fire, it's all over. Everything I own will bust right into flames and I'll have to start all over putting my life into perspective. And I like that word— perspective—it can make something sound a lot more important than it is. Not that I don't value my life, because I do, but sometimes I wish that I could spread it all out on a piece of paper and take some Wite-out to it. Larry Cross would be the first to go. I tell people (if they happen to ask) that he does odd jobs in California. I don't tell them that I think he's a drug pusher because that would stick and get turned right back around and follow me like gum on a shoe wherever I may go in this life. They'd say, "That's Maureen Dummer, who works as a teller and used to live with a pusher down in Fuquay-Varina," and I can't have that. Now people just say things like "That's Maureen Dummer, who works down there at the First Union Bank; she's the teller with the strawberry-blond hair that looks a tiny bit like Krystle Carrington off 'Dynasty.' She has a cute little girl by the name of Larrette. No, she's a single parent."

If my daddy wasn't already dead, I'd want to kill him for not changing our name legal to something else. "She's Dummer!" That's what children said to me at school, and I know they'll do it to Larrette if I don't get married and have whoever adopt her first. Some things never change—children teasing other children and people taking a little information and turning it all around and sticking it to you like a wad of Juicy Fruit. We can't chew gum while on the window or smoke cigarettes. "It looks bad," my boss, Mr. Crown, says, and I could bust his crown. I work right here and yet when I decided to get me a Visa card, I had one hell of a time. To get a card you have to show that you charge up a blue streak, that you owe money here and there. "I have always paid what I owe," I told him, only to be told that I have no credit. I went and got me a micro-wave and a washer and dryer on time so I could owe some money and get a card so I'd be able to write a check in the grocery store. I probably couldn't have done that if Earl Taylor hadn't been working there in Sears and hadn't been taken with me. He asked me to go for dinner and I asked him to let me charge and pay on time and we shook on

it, ate Chinese food, and the next day my things were delivered. Larrette had a fit over those big pasteboard boxes.
I've been going out with Earl ever since.

I figure Larry Cross has himself one of those sticks that'll
beep if he's walking there on the strand and happens upon
some change. That's what he does all day long, that and
take pills and sell pills and do sex stuff. I'd be stupid to tell
all of that and I am not stupid. "Why did you take a check
that wasn't endorsed?" Mr. Crown asked me first thing this
morning, those other girls studying their papers like they
were still in school, thankful to death, I know, that I had
done it and not them. "You're not stupid, Maureen," he
said and I said, "No, sir, I am not." I can admit to a mistake; it's easy if you've got the right perspective on it all;
such as, Mr. Crown sits in a leather chair all day long and
never once has to touch a nasty old piece of money that has
been God only knows where and might have some disease
on it. If Mr. Crown sat here at the window and saw what's
going in and out of this place, who's bouncing and who's
scrimping, then he'd be likely to mess up occasionally, too.
"You've got to concentrate, Maureen."
And I'm certainly not stupid. Stupid would be if I told all
I know about Larry Cross. Sex stuff, that's the only reason I
got hooked up with Larry Cross to begin with and that ties
right in with that Spanish tan and hairy chest because he
was right good-looking in an apelike way. He looked like

those little he-men dolls, except his hair was black and he had a real full beard like that man on "Little House on the Prairie," not Little Joe Cartwright but that other man that lived all alone most of the shows and dated that school-teacher a time or two. Larry Cross was all right but I'm not stupid. I mean, why would I marry trash? Especially trash with a last name that isn't much better than my own. Taylor—that's Earl's last name and one I'm thinking I could probably live with.

Sometimes my mouth gets all worked up with saliva handling all this money. I am not good with money. That's my biggest fault. It's a fault I've always had; if it's in my wallet then I just naturally think it's for spending and that outlet mall can get me in a whip-snap. Larry Cross had the fault of spending worse than me. If I was still with him he'd probably be sitting in the living room of that condo with those long legs stretched out on the coffee table and he'd be wearing nothing but some bathing trunks, letting the kitchen burn down, while he drew up a plan of how I could slip a little money every now and then. Embezzle is the word and I'd put my body on the street before I ever did that. I've got Larrette to think of but would he have ever thought of Larrette as something other than a Frisbee fetcher? No, no way. "I am not a dog," I told him when he'd say, "Honey, can you reach that Frisbee?" and that Frisbee about a hundred feet from where I was sitting. "If I had a rubber arm," I'd say.

I'd like for somebody to run my business. It isn't that I'm not into liberation. God knows, you can just look at me and know that I am; you can know by my credit cards in my wallet, Visa, Ivey's, and Texaco. But still, it would be so nice to have somebody run my business, somebody who would say, "Now, honey, look here. You just thought you threw out your W-2 and here it is right under this stack of Christmas cards that you forgot to open." Take Earl Taylor, for example.

"I'd rather not," Eleanore always says when I say that. Eleanore is a teacher's aide in the elementary school and that has slowed her thoughts down some, though she's real good with Larrette. She was the first one to get Larrette to say kitty and to learn to meow.

Eleanore goes with a man who already has a wife, so she can't really talk much. She only gets to see him every now and then at the Ramada Inn in Apex. She thinks he's going to leave that wife that drives a mini-van and heads up Easter Seals every year, and those two babies and that house that looks like a little fairy cottage out in a nice part of town for her. She likes for me to get in my car and drive her by that house late at night and she'll say things like, "Yep, TV's on. I knew he'd be watching TV. I know that man like the back of my hand. He's sitting up late watching the TV so he doesn't have to get in the bed with *her*." Eleanore doesn't know any better. She's two years older than me, thirty-one, but she doesn't know a bit better.

She hasn't had life's lessons taught to her like I did staying in Fuquay with Larry Cross. I shouldn't encourage that. I shouldn't even drive her past that house for her to fill her head with stories, but sometimes it's fun. Sometimes we say we're going to disguise ourselves in case a cop should pull us over right there in front of that house, so I put on some sunglasses and tie a scarf to my head and I must admit that I like to do that because it makes me feel like I look a little like Susan Hayward and so I say things like "I Want to Live!" or "I'd Climb the Highest Mountain!" or "Let's ride on 'Back Street'!" and Eleanore will take it in her head that if she wears a gingham shirt and sunglasses that she looks like Doris Day and she will say, "Lover Come Back!" and "Where Were You When the Lights Went Out?" We have some fun times, me and Eleanore, and we always have, but then I have to get serious.

"Eleanore, you might as well look elsewhere," I say, and she rolls those big blue eyes that are common among us Dummers (her mama was a Dummer) like I might be a little breeze whistling past her ear. You can't tell her.

"I don't know what you see in Earl Taylor," she says. "Earl Taylor is a little nerd." I can see where she gets that. I can. To somebody who doesn't know Earl Taylor like I know him, he might look that way because of the way his hair is so thin and weak-looking and those glasses that he has to wear. But Earl is smart and that's how he looks. He looks like somebody that can handle figures and money. Now, he doesn't make a bed slope way off to one side or creak and groan like Larry Cross did, and he doesn't make *me* creak and groan like Larry Cross did. As a matter of fact, Earl can get in and out of a bed and you don't even know he's been there. Now, I don't want anybody getting me wrong because there is no such goings on in that condo with Larrette right there in the same dwelling. The only time that Earl and me have actually spent the night until dawn in a bed together was the weekend that Eleanore kept Larrette and we went down to Ocean Drive, which might as well be Myrtle Beach the way it's grown. "Myrtle Beach, Ocean Drive, they run right together," Earl said, and he was right. I couldn't have drawn a line between the two if I had had to. Other than that, we just pop over to Earl's place every now and then. He has a bed that's just on a frame with a green glass-shaded floor lamp right there beside it so he can read in bed. Earl likes that green glass lamp shade because it's related to his profession, but that green glass is the only adornment of any kind that he owns. Plain. It's all real plain, but it's clean.

Earl is smarter than Larry Cross was even before he killed off so many brain cells. I looked it all up in the library while I was in Fuquay. I looked up drugs and one thing led to another till pretty soon I was reading on brain cells and come to find out that once they're dead, they're dead. As dead as that rubber tree that Eleanore has in her living room thinking it's gonna bush back and be something. Larry Cross will never be something.

Earl Taylor is already something; he's in charge of

finances at Sears. He banks here with us and so I've seen his savings account and it is a fat one. That doesn't surprise me a bit because it's obvious that he doesn't throw money away; it's obvious by the way that his place is so plain and the way that he wears clothes that mix and mingle to the degree that it seems like he has on the same outfit every single day. When I think of Earl, I think khaki and oxford cloth. When I think of Larry Cross, I think Levi's and loud Hawaiian shirts, and loud-colored swim trunks and gym shorts. Flashy—Larry Cross is flashy with the money he doesn't have and that little Spitfire convertible in bright orange that I was forever needing to jump with my VW Bug. Earl Taylor drives a Mazda, a nice, neat, plain, navy Mazda that he vacuums on a regular basis. Sometimes we'll be on our way out to eat and Earl will whip right in the Drive-Thru Klean-a-Kar and pop a quarter into that vacuum and run over things. He took the shoes right off of my feet and cleaned up the bottom of them for me. Night and day. That's what Larry Cross and Earl Taylor are.

"You are making a big mistake if you get hooked up with him," Eleanore tells me. Eleanore comes over every Tuesday night and fills my washer full of slinky nightwear she only wears in Apex. "What you like about Earl is how he isn't like Larry. Now tell the truth." Eleanore always says that, "Now tell the truth," but she only wants your truth; she turns a deaf ear if you discuss her truth.

"That's not the reason," I tell her. "Earl is a good businessman."

"And Larry Cross was not," she'll snap, though I know he must've done all right to have had that stream of weirdos coming by all the time. Of course, I never say that.

"Earl is as neat as a pin."

"And Larry Cross was a slob," she says and doesn't even pause to breathe. "And I'll give you the last one. Larry Cross, as worthless as he is, is good-looking and Earl Taylor is not."

"Beauty is in the eye of the beholder," I tell her, though I know better. "Beauty is only skin deep and Earl goes through and through."

"How? Name one way." Eleanore is so persistent with perspectives other than her own.

"He fixed it so I could get myself established with credit."

"That's his job. Name another."

"He's sweet to Larrette," I say, and Eleanore can't deny that one because she's never seen Earl around Larrette that much.

"What does he think about the way you spend money? What does he think about the way you order just about everything that Yield House has to offer?"

"Earl doesn't care," I tell her and that's true. Half the time Earl doesn't even notice, which is, I guess, another difference between him and Larry Cross. If Larry Cross was to slap those long legs up on a brand new butler's table, he'd at least notice. He'd say, "Where'd you get this?" and I'd say what I always said, "At the getting place." Larry Cross didn't know a thing about the business because I made the money and I paid the bills and I just about lost my mind doing it.

There's a woman leaning out of her car window right now with a check and a deposit slip in her hand and a diamond that would make anybody proud sparkling on her finger. "Hi, Gail, how are you today?" I say before I even open the drawer and pull it back in. I know her without even looking at the name on her deposit slip because she comes in every Monday with her husband's check that he got on Friday. William Anderson, MD, and her name is right there under his, Gail Mason-Anderson. That check is something, too; I bet the United States of this country makes more off of one of William Anderson's checks than I make in four months gross. They live on Winona in a two-story house that's got a pool in the back. I know because I looked for that house when I rode Eleanore by to see whether or not her boyfriend was really out of town on the weekend when they were supposed to meet in Apex. He wasn't. He was right there in his backyard, wearing an apron and carrying barbecue tongs, with cars lined up on either side of the street. "He's out of town all right," I told Eleanore.

"It's *her*," she said. "*She* makes him do all these social things with people he can't stand. He does it to keep her off his back just a little bit."

"He lied," I told her.

"He didn't want me to be hurt by it." She had taken off

her Doris Day glasses and wiped her eyes. "He's protective of my feelings."

I sang "Que Será, Será" but it didn't perk her up. It made her mad, to be perfectly honest, and so she lit into Earl Taylor like a fly on you know what, because that's what she always does when her own life is going bad and she has no choice but to admit it.

"I hope you had a nice weekend, Gail," I say when I slip back that deposit slip minus the 150 dollars that I put in one of our little envelopes. Now she's going over to Kroger's and put that 150 dollars to use, does it every Monday. I know Gail Mason-Anderson like the back of my hand.

"I did," Gail says, but she doesn't look at me because she's checking to make sure that I gave her the 150 she requested. Seven twenties and one ten, can't get any closer than that, though I'm not offended when people do that. I'm glad people sit right there and check it because if she got to Kroger's and then came back it would be her word against mine and Mr. Crown would chew me out whether I was in the right or wrong. "Think of the ways people could trick us out of money," I told him one day and it's the truth. There are numerous ways that you might trick a teller out of money and it is my job to keep that from happening. Not that I think Gail Mason-Anderson would do any such thing. She doesn't have to. I bet she and William Anderson have a man who looks a lot like Earl Taylor to just figure it all up for them.

I like to think of having a hyphenated name myself. Maureen Dummer hyphen something. Maureen Dummer-Taylor with right above it Earl Sinco Taylor. "Your name sounds like a plumbing product," I told him, only to find that I had hurt his feelings. Sinco is a name from somewhere in his mama's family, and since his mama is dead, it made him real defensive that I should laugh at that name.

"Thank you," Gail says. I read her lips because I've already cut off my speaker. She drives a diesel-powered Audi, and it wrecks my ears to hear it going on and on and ricocheting off the little drive-through area. I just nod and watch Gail Mason-Anderson go straight to Kroger's.

Eighty-five degrees F and 11:37. I decide I'll go and take my lunch hour a little early. I do that every now and again when it's important like today when I am not going to Eckerd's and order a grilled cheese but am going home and make sure there's no fire started. It will take the whole hour but it's the only way that I can stay in my seat the rest of the afternoon, not to mention that I have got a little nic craving that I can't hold off anymore. I don't even bring my cigarettes into this building because it would be such a temptation, not to mention that Trish, who sits at the other little opening, wears one of those badges that has a picture with a slash through it. A picture paints a thousand words and I don't need to be hit over the head. Trish has a husband and that's how she can afford to be so outspoken. She hates cigarettes and loves manatees, the Cape

Hatteras lighthouse, Statue of Liberty, 96LITE, and Jesus. You can read it all right there on the bumper of her car. I personally would not open my life like a book to the world. I have a sticker that says GET OFF MY REAR! and that's all. Trish brakes for animals but won't answer a person when they say they're going to lunch. She just looks at the clock machine and rolls her eyes like I'm going to abuse the system and stay out until one instead of returning at 12:53, which will be exactly an hour from when my car exits the lot, give or take a few minutes. Trish supports the system, the public schools, the Little Theater, the President, and whales. All I know about Trish I've learned right off of that car. Her savings account shared with Edward Hunter cannot touch the savings account of Gail Mason-Anderson and William or that of Earl Sinco Taylor.

Now I feel like I can't get this Bug to go fast enough. It's like all of a sudden I'm in a panic to see my condo still standing with my potted geranium on the front stoop and my straw hat with lacy ribbons on my door. Welcome and welcome relief it is when I turn this corner a little and see it. What I don't welcome is Eleanore standing on the sidewalk with what looks like catsup or poster paints there on the front of her blouse that I gave her for her birthday two years ago. That blouse not only is out of style but if it was in style it is far too frilly for a Monday morning in the elementary school. "It's a church blouse," I told her and she gave me the Dummer eye.

Eleanore has always taken things personally. The time I told her that there is a difference in the country look that is authentic and the country look that is a hodge-podge of too much of a good thing, she took it personally and I certainly didn't mean it for her personally, even though she does not need one more rooster looking like it's about to crow tacked up on her kitchen wall. I think it's symbolic that she's so into roosters, all that strutting and taking hold of every hen and that's not even touching the biblical symbol, three crows and you're out.

"Where have you been?" she asks just as soon as I step out of the Bug and this heat hits my head like a ton of bricks. "I've been waiting forever."

"I didn't know you were coming," I tell her. I do more than tell her. I state it like the fact that it is. This isn't the first time Eleanore has pulled such a visit only to turn it around and make it my fault that she's been waiting. And where else would I have been but at the bank, here in this navy linen suit with matching pumps, and little canvas clutch? Every fiber of my Monday-through-Friday wardrobe says "teller."

I get up close and I can see that Eleanore has been crying, and it takes me a second to remember why I trucked clean across town home—the Mr. Coffee. "Come on in," I tell her. "I'm afraid I left the Mr. Coffee on." Eleanore follows me in and just about falls down on a Fisher-Price bathtub frog which Larrette meows to. We both have tried to teach her to say "frog" but she is as stubborn in that way as Larry Cross. "Gotta love that Squeaky," he used to say to me and throw those gorilla arms around my hips. He called me Squeaky because he thought I looked like that woman that tried to shoot Gerald Ford that time, and I don't. "I love my Squeaky," he would say because he didn't have much sense, but God, just the thought of that bed breaking down and not even fazing that man makes my heart skip a beat or two.

It's on. Plugged in and on, that pot bottom dried into nothing but crisp brown sludge. "I did it," I say to Eleanore, who is at that kitchen table with a Kleenex up to her face. "Thank God, there wasn't a fire."

"He's gone back to his wife," Eleanore sobs. "Don't you say 'I told you so' one time since I'm going ahead and saying it for you."

I'm a little confused since to my knowledge he never left his wife to begin with. "I didn't know he had left her."

"He left her a year ago. He left her that first night we stayed in Apex and he told me that he loved me like he had never loved anybody." Eleanore primps up and sobs again, wiping her mascara on my linen pineapple-print napkins. "I mean he still lived there, with *her*, but it was me he loved." I listen to Eleanore telling the details of it all while the Mr. Coffee pot cools enough that I can rinse out that crud, but while Eleanore is going on my mind is thinking over that word *love*, and how it is used and misused and abused. Earl Taylor has said that word one time when it referred to me. Once, and I'm thinking that that isn't good enough. I'm thinking of "Love my Squeaky" and Larry Cross might have meant it as much as if he'd said "Love my Carpet," but still he said it.

"He said if he could live his life over that he would be with me," Eleanore says and looks up from my napkin, black smudges all over it. "He said it on the phone and then there came a sweetheart rose to the school office. No card. It's right out there in my car if you want to see it."

"I don't need to see it," I tell her. "But what would you have done if I hadn't come to lunch?"

"You usually do come to lunch," Eleanore says. "You're usually here by eleven-thirty."

"Well," I say because I've never thought that she would busy herself to pick up on my daily patterns.

"Mr. Coffee, iron, oven, it's always something." Eleanore goes over and gets Larrette's little frog and hugs it. It squeaks. I hear a *squeak squeaky* loud and clear, Larry Cross and bedsprings that Earl Taylor couldn't squeak if he did a somersault with bricks tied around his neck. "I know you like a book, Maureen."

"I reckon you do," I say and rinse that napkin out in cold water and a little Stanley spot remover. "Must be the Dummer in us."

"I know Tuesday is my wash night but I was wondering if I could come over tonight instead," Eleanore says, and there's no way I can tell her no. It's my night to cook a little something for me and Earl and for us to watch "Cagney and Lacy" and I don't even care. I don't even care that

I'm going to break that pattern starting tonight, and if Gail Mason-Anderson had some sense she'd break *her* habit and occasionally go to Harris Teeter, where they've got fresh seafood coming in by the barrel.

"I think that's a good idea," I tell her and go over to touch that pot to see if it's cooled down enough that it won't crack.

"What about Earl Taylor?"

"Well, Earl Taylor can do something else. Earl Taylor can vacuum his Mazda, for example." I run warm water first and take my Tuffy pad to the bottom of that pot. "Let's go to Harris Teeter and buy some scallops," I say when I'm so happy that pot doesn't crack and splinter in my hands. "Let's get some wine and some cheese, not dairy counter but deli cheese. And let's go in Ivey's and buy you some cologne and a blouse that's in style." Eleanore has taken that personally I can tell, but she is too upset to argue.

"I can't buy a new blouse," she says, her eyes watering again. "I don't get paid until the end of the month."

"We'll just put it right on my card," I tell her. "If it weren't for you, Larrette probably wouldn't be speaking at all. I'm expecting any day now that she's going to get up and say frog and Kermit and everything else that goes with it." That pot comes clean as a whistle and while it's air drying, I go and call Trish to say I won't be back.

"I've taken ill," I tell her. "I could barely get myself to the bathroom."

"Didn't you take ill last week?" Trish asks, and I figure

she doesn't even deserve an answer. "Are you expecting?" Trish asks, and I can't help but laugh a little in between making my voice sound sick, low and slow and sick; I've always been able to make my voice that way instinctively. I'd do my voice that way and Larry Cross would make all kinds of promises that he never kept. I did it to Earl once and he didn't even notice. I'd rather be told a lie than nothing at all, and Trish should feel that way, too.

"I may be," I tell her. "You might have hit the nail on the head, Trish."

"Don't you date Earl Taylor down at Sears?"

"Yes, yes I do." I tell Trish that I think I'll go to the doctor and that I'll see her in the morning. But first I tell her that my cousin, Eleanore Tripper, works in the public schools and once saw a manatee down in Florida. This is the most me and Trish have ever even conversed. Now I call Earl to say I'm tied up for the evening.

"But it's Monday," he says. " 'Cagney and Lacy' comes on." He states all that as a fact and I realize that all Earl has ever done to me is state facts. A fact is just a base, a foot in the door, to perspectives and instincts. Earl Taylor has got a lot to learn. "What am I going to do?" he asks, and I can tell he is in a hurry because he is not one to squander work time.

"You could vacuum your car."

"I did that yesterday."

"You could go shopping."

"I don't need anything," he says, which is a lie, though he thinks it is the truth. He needs some pictures on his wall and to rip up that shag carpet, finish those floors, and buy himself some pretty braided rugs. He could use a grapevine wreath, a shower curtain other than a white cheapo liner, and some pretty towels that match. He needs a headboard and an Alexander Julian shirt and some contact lenses and some hair conditioner that'll give body. He needs a body, a membership at a spa, barbells.

"Oh now, Earl," I say. "I bet if you went to the mall you could find some things you need."

"I don't believe in just going out and spending money," he says and sounds a little exasperated, and I know just how he's looking with that exasperation, red-eared, bleary-eyed, and dull in an official way. "And I really can't talk. I'm working. You should be working."

I start to tell him that he could gain some weight but I don't. I just hang up, put on my sunglasses, and go get my scarf to tie on my head. "Let's wear our outfits to the Harris Teeter," I say. "No telling who might see me and run by First Union to tell it." For the first time Eleanore smiles; it's a weak smile and I know the whole night is going to be potato chips and Cokes and her tears working like a faucet. She puts on her glasses and says she'll pretend she's wearing a gingham shirt, and off we go once I check to make sure the hot rollers or Larrette's vaporizer aren't still going.

We pass the North Carolina Bank and Trust and their

sign says 88 F and I can believe it. It's hot and clear and feels so good I could stretch out like a dog with little to no clothes on and imagine Larry Cross out walking some strand with his beeper stick and thinking of me, thinking that he was a fool not to know what he had when he had it. I know that's probably a lie but right now I like to believe it. Right now I can believe in that lie and keep it all in perspective.

"Lover Come Back," Eleanore says, and though the tears come to her eyes, she sings a little of "Que Será, Será." Will I be pretty? Will I be rich?

"I Want to Live," I tell her, and I toot that VW horn to do a "Que Será, Será," and that's no lie. We pass by First Union and I hold my head high since I've got on my costume, and I don't even look to see what time of day it may be and I don't even care that that fair-skinned arm of mine hanging out the window could get burned to a Jane Eyre crisp on a day like today. And I wouldn't trade places with Trish sitting there under the green lights, or Gail Mason-Anderson with her cabinets overflowed with Kroger bags or her purse filled up with deposit slips with my initials, or my cousin Eleanore, who is staring out the window through a steady stream of tears while she tries to get a better perspective on things.

Departures

Anna Craven has been going places all alone for three years now—airports, shopping malls, fairs, political rallies, any place where she can be surrounded by people without having to interact with any of them. She only works two days a week (could be retired if she desired), so it's not like the outings rob anybody or anything. Her children are scattered off in every direction living their own lives, and her time is something that can't easily be filled with cooking or talking on the phone.

"Why don't you watch TV?" they asked over the holidays and pointed to that great big set they had given her the year before. "I do," she told them and did not try to explain how there was more drama to be seen in public places.

"It's not healthy, all this time alone," her son-in-law, the therapist, had said, "There are plenty of other women who are . . ." He faltered for the right words, *widows? all alone?* "Why are you punishing yourself?"

Punishment. The punishment was that Walter was no longer with her—period, the end. Divorcées go out for drinks and dancing—even the ones her age—but the *widows*, the *all alone*, are supposed to drink coffee and play mah-jongg, sing in the church choir, never think about or wish for intercourse other than of a verbal or spiritual nature. Nobody even uses that word in front of a widow—intercourse. Sometimes she wants to tell her son-in-law the therapist that that is punishment; perfectly good solid words reduced to nothing. Punishment was that day three years ago when she got the call that Walter had died. He was on business, the West Coast, his last looks fastened on some awful hotel furniture, the telephone cord beyond his reach.

She had just gotten home from the elementary school when the call came. The kids at school called her "the traveling musician" because she made her rounds to each class once a week. Her music lessons were usually related to the closest season or holiday at hand, but she also had her favorites to be sung in between these times, songs such as "Born Free" or "I Left My Heart in San Francisco." That one was wonderful to hear, a chorus of little high-pitched voices singing words they did not fully understand, much like "Mares Eat Oats."

That particular day she had spent the classtime singing "Gobble Gobble Turkey" while the students drew their
own versions of the first Thanksgiving, turkeys whose tail
feathers were the outline of a hand, each finger colored a
different hue. Her mind had been on the upcoming holiday
and what kind of sleeping arrangements they would make
for the growing family. Her daughter, Carol (wife of the
therapist), was pregnant with their second child. Carol had
said that Kim, the fifteen-month-old, only ate pizza crust
and that Trey (the therapist, whose name was William
Bradford *the third*) said that it was important they let Kim
eat her way through this, that if they used any force of
any kind she might never eat vegetables. Anna and Walter
had sat up many late nights talking about how absurd their
ideas were, how it seemed such a shame that all of Kim's
toys as an infant had been in basic black and white because
this is what stimulates newborns. Anna kept wanting to remove the odd dull toys and replace them with fluffy pastel
bears and cats.

Trey had videotaped every minute detail of childbirth.
He carried the placenta home in a lawn-and-garden bag;
(though curious, Anna never asked what they *did* with
it). He studied the child's every movement, quick to tell
anyone who would listen what Kim could and could not
see, could and could not know. Walter's greatest fear had
been that they would have a son and name him something
something the fourth.

"And then what?" Walter had asked off and on for a

month. "Will they call him Quar?" He tossed his travel kit into his suitcase, then stretched out on the bed and laughed. "Or queer?" He shook his head, hands clasped behind his neck as he watched her put on her nightgown. They had always done that, locked looks in the mirror as she undressed for bed.

Their older son, Ben, had just gotten his divorce and was going to bring the new girlfriend and her four-year-old. The girlfriend had told Anna in their one and only conversation on the telephone that she had had a child on her own because she had not yet met the right man. "Little did I know the right man was still married at the time," she had said and laughed, Ben chuckling with her in the background. "Divorce is so prevalent I knew I'd find somebody eventually; you know, somebody who could be a father figure, not of course that I think a father figure is important. They aren't. Men are not always necessary." *Can you imagine?* Anna had asked after hanging up the phone. *The gall. The poor taste.* Walter said he would like to put this woman and Trey in a room and lock the door, take bets on which one would survive the night. Anna said she'd just like to tell them not to come, but Walter talked her out of it; he said it would be one of those occasions they would enjoy *after* the fact.

At the time, their younger son, Wayne, seemed to be the only sane one. He was just out of law school and studying for the bar. Except for an earring in one ear, he was classically clean-cut with a wardrobe of 100 percent cotton and name brands. The earring—a tiny diamond chip like a star—prompted Walter to say he had a hole in his head, but it was a joke. They talked a lot about how Wayne had the most sense. How he was the caring child. "A little depressed, maybe," Walter said often. "But he'll pull out of it. Got a lot of pressure on him."

She had been thinking about the children coming home when the phone rang. She was standing in the kitchen, one crayoned turkey folded neatly in her purse. She was thinking about stuffing—in the bird or out of the bird? Carol (who said that pregnancy had brought with it a great distaste for poultry) liked the stuffing (or had liked it) crumbling out from the bird; Walter preferred it fixed in a pan (dressing it is called) because he said he hated the thought of scooping around inside the bird. He said he couldn't stand to think of either end of the creature and refused to eat giblet gravy because he did not eat any of the *working parts*, no *organs*. Trey did not like any two items touching on his plate and often had to have lots of separate little bowls like in a cafeteria. He also talked a great deal about *roughage*. She was envisioning both—emptying the turkey out of Walter's vision—but also having a nice pan of dressing cut into squares. She would prepare a huge salad and some bran muffins and, if that wasn't enough roughage, would offer a Metamucil cocktail. The phone ringing was an interruption, and she was slow to grasp the purpose of the call.

Oh dear God, she remembers saying and, with the phone cradled under her chin, had slowly and systematically shredded that paper turkey. She had stood, not knowing what to do with her hands or with the turkey that was thawing on the counter. That very morning she had changed the sheets on the bed. The pillows were fluffed to his liking, *TV Guide* was placed there on the nightstand, clean pajamas were folded in his drawer. The thought of their bedroom, the minute details of their world, made her feel unbearably alive. Walter's raincoat was hanging there in the hall. She ran past it to the stairs. Their bedroom was just as she had left it that morning when the sun streamed through the window, and she was so sorry that she had not waited to wash, so terribly sorry that she did not have his pajamas and the sheets left on the bed from day before yesterday.

She was standing in the kitchen when the phone rang and then it seemed that within minutes they were all there, these people, these children she had birthed while unconscious, with Walter in the waiting room chain-smoking with the other men—these children they had conceived in the darkness of their bed: Carol in that tiny studio apartment overlooking the A&P parking lot; Ben, in their first house, the small two-bedroom Cape Cod where she left behind a rosebush she had brought from her grandmother's house (when she went back and requested it, the new owners refused); and finally Wayne, in a rented cottage one row back from the ocean, salt wind whipping the sticky draperies.

Ben came home without the girlfriend, and the only thing Anna said to him that night was "How dare you ask to bring such a trollop to my house when we still haven't gotten over your divorce?" She told Trey and Carol that if they didn't stop talking about gastrointestinal and psychiatric things that they would have to get out, they were making her sick. She told Wayne that she wished he'd pierce his other ear so that she didn't have the inclination when looking at him to tilt her head in attempt to make up for his lack of symmetry. She asked him please to guard her bedroom door so that no one would come in to talk to her or to try and get her to talk or eat or turn on a light. She didn't cook a turkey; she didn't leave her room. It was the lousiest Thanksgiving known to man.

Walter's favorite movie was *Rear Window*. He said the movie reminded him of them and the way they sat on the balcony of that rented beach house and watched the lights in the row of houses across the way. They had gone to the same house every summer when the kids were growing up. It was not a big cottage, just a small white wooden house up on tall spindly-looking pilings; it was one row back from the ocean, a short walk to the pier.

"Well, I'm no Grace Kelly," Anna had said and laughed. The first year they had watched an older couple across the way; they had laughed at the way it seemed they dressed for dinner, the woman in a floor-length floral skirt and the man in a white jacket and white shoes. "Like Pat Boone," Walter had howled. He was only thirty-six then and his skin was a dark tan. "Imagine getting dressed up like that at the beach."

The couple became a joke for them, their own *Rear Window*. Each day Anna and Walter would sit on the beach (she under a big striped umbrella) while Ben and Carol played in the sand and at the edge of the water. They would take turns glancing up at the big weathered house, each anxious to be the first to spy the couple, but the front shades remained drawn throughout the day. "Maybe they're vampires," Walter whispered and stretched out beside her, his skin sandy and sunburned. "Maybe they're spying on *us* right now and they don't want us to meet because then we'll all just have ordinary boring vacations."

"It's not so boring," she said and yawned. "I love doing nothing." It was a wonderful feeling to collect their things and head up over the huge white dunes in the early afternoon. The kids ran ahead, stopping to examine shells and the wild roses that grew close by, while she and Walter followed, drawn by the thought of a cool shower and a nap. Once when Wayne was nine he had asked them *why* they decided to have him. Anna looked over at Walter but he didn't look like someone on the verge of speaking. "We wanted another baby," she said. "That's all we could talk about that summer at the beach, how we wanted another baby." Walter grinned at her, eyebrows raised with the silent truth: they had been delirious with joy when the children finally closed their little eyes and mouths and slept like lambs. They had been careless, wild, and reckless, thinking that if something *did* happen they'd deal with it later. The nearest drugstore was a twenty-minute drive, and there just wasn't always time enough to be prepared.

It was in the late afternoons, when the beach was empty, that the couple strolled out, cocktail glasses in hand, and sat on their deck. When the sun set, they got in the car and left for their late-night dinner. Anna and Walter imagined them driving over to a friend's house, maybe one of the large antebellum homes just inland, where they would sit at a long polished table and sip champagne. By now Walter had nicknamed them "the Vanderbilts." With the children tucked in, Anna and Walter sat on their own tiny deck and waited for the Vanderbilts' return. They took turns using an old telescope to zero in on the lights of the pier; one night they saw a man catch what looked like a shark before a circle of people blocked their view. Another night they spotted a young couple kissing below the bait shop,

the woman's back pressed against one of the creosote pilings. Walter said that at least one of them was married, an
illicit affair; Anna said they were teenagers trying things
out for the first time. They would have placed a bet except
there was no way of learning the truth. They sat with their
telescope, the transistor radio playing, until the headlights
came around a curve. The Vanderbilts always returned just
before midnight. Their lights went out half an hour later.

The last day of vacation, Anna suggested they follow the
couple on their nightly outing. As soon as they appeared on
their deck, cocktails in hand, Anna started getting ready.
Carol and Ben were in the back seat singing and screaming
(they were going to get ice cream), and Anna and Walter
took turns fiddling with something (he under the hood, she
running back into the house) until the couple across the
street prepared to leave. Finally, the Lincoln pulled out and
they let them get a good block down the road before they
pulled out and began following. Anna was excited, ready
for a lengthy expedition that might take them who knew
where, only to be disappointed five minutes later when
the car turned into Brady's Seafood, an old establishment
adorned with plastic fish and nets and offering fried food
galore. Walter turned off the headlights, the car still idling,
as they watched the man walk around to open her door.
Her floral evening skirt glistened under the streetlights as
they walked to the big glass door. Inside they would be met
by the glare of ceiling lights on Formica, the smell of fish
and a reheated grease vat.

"Disappointed?" Walter asked as he turned their station wagon around, flipped on the headlights, and drove to the Tastee Freeze next to a Putt-Putt Golf range. They sat on a bench and let the kids run around on the little green course. "They deserve better, don't they?" he asked, and she suddenly felt very defensive of these complete strangers. "Maybe they're happy," she said. "What do we know?" It became a quote used often over the next twenty-five years. It's what Walter always said to her (reminding her) if she commented on someone else's life. It's what she imagines people are saying about *her* life now that she is all alone in public places.

She has spent three years without Walter and she has adjusted to the shock. She has gotten used to the largeness of the bed, the quiet ticking of the clocks that his snores and breathing had always hidden. Still, she comes to loud public places to absorb the emotions. People in airports cry and hug, *Look at you!*; they lean and wave. *I thought you'd never get here!* People at political rallies or marches smile and cheer one another on as if there is a relationship there. All you have to do is clap at the right time, raise your hand in affirmation or rejection at the right time. People in the mall are absorbed into the fluorescent lights and water fountains.

Now, Carol has had *another* boy (Brandon) to follow that first one (William the Fourth) and stays at home with them while Trey sits and records people's problems out in his black-and-white office, which used to be the garage. Carol wears children like most people wear arms and legs. She is already talking about having another. Anna can't imagine that Carol and Trey have ever done anything reckless. All of these children are planned, one right after another. Carol never talks about anything else these days. Carol never says, "What do you miss most about Dad? What would be your pick of a day if you could have one?" Instead, Carol says, "Trey and I have got to get a new diaper service, we're dissatisfied with the way this service folds—there's always a wrinkle in the front. We fear they use really strong detergents, too, else how do they get the diapers so white? Trey says I can just keep searching until I find the perfect service, no matter the cost, isn't he wonderful?" And Anna says, "Well, Carol, if I could have any day with your father, I'd pick a day in July that very summer that we surprised ourselves and I got pregnant with Wayne. Your dad would tiptoe to look in on you and Ben to make sure you were completely out, and then he'd come flying back and lock our door, jump in the bed and there we'd be, laughing and whispering and doing anything we pleased. If I could've bought Huggies, I would've."

"Mom, I can't let Kim and William and Brandon eat canned spaghetti. When you said you had spaghetti, I thought you meant *real* spaghetti." Carol stands there, her eyes as blue as Walter's, her nose with the same slope. She used to eat canned spaghetti all the time. Anna looks at the open can and puts it on the counter. She wants to say, *Your father and I would go after each other like crazed rabbits and we wouldn't stop until we fell out with exhaustion or until one of you started calling from the other room, whichever came first,* but instead she tells her that if she wants *real* spaghetti, that if Chef Boyardee, who has been around longer than Trey, is not good enough, then she'll have to do her own shopping and cooking.

Ben, after a series of live-in girlfriends, met and married somebody who looked and sounded just like all the others. They moved to Alaska, where he teaches history. His wife teaches arts and crafts in the prison there and for Christmas sent Anna a pendant carved from ivory. It's an awkward elephant, so large it would knock her out if she forgot and bent over too fast, that is *if* she ever wore it. Terri (the wife whom she has met only once) sent a history of this elephant: *This was carved by a reformed alcoholic named Ike who is serving a life sentence for murdering his wife, mother, and child. Ike has found religion and sees his art as a manifestation of his cleansed soul. He is a new man.* Though the children at school would probably love this atrocity the same way they love when she wears her loud parrot pin, Anna will not touch it with a ten-foot pole. Imagine, writing to *tell* her such a thing. Didn't they know that she would only stare at the misshapen piece of junk and ask why such a man is living and breathing and whittling his animal tusks while Walter, who was the epitome of sanity and goodness, is gone? Were it not for completely alienating her son and his free-spirited wife, she would throw it out in the trash. Instead, she has it boxed up and placed in the drawer where she keeps a photo from Ben's *first* marriage, the other wife, a cute quiet conventional woman who wanted to settle and spend her life somewhere. "That's not so much for her to ask," Walter had told Ben when he announced with anger that they were separated, that she was asking too much of him. "What is it you're looking for?"

Wayne, after only a few months practicing law, decided that it was not for him and went back to get an MBA. Now he's considering a CPA. What happened to the normal child? She keeps asking the question and wishing Walter could answer. Anna recently asked Wayne why he didn't drive his BMW while eating a BLT to the YMCA for a little R&R or better yet, why didn't he find a nice young woman who could give him some TLC? What she has found out most recently is that Wayne is more interested in finding a nice young man and she thinks she can live with all that. She is convinced she can live with just about anything. It's what she can't live without that poses a problem.

The summer after Wayne was born they went back to the small cottage. Anna spent most of the vacation up on the screened-in porch with Wayne in her arms, his tiny body shielded from the salty breeze by a cotton blanket. It was midweek before they saw any lights on in the house across the way. There were several cars in the drive (the Lincoln was in the garage but they never saw it move), and the beach in front of the house was peppered with children of all ages. Anna had a lot of time to watch while Walter was out swimming with the kids and she was left behind to the shade of the porch. All day long people came and went, but no sign of the couple from the year before other than their car.

Finally, late one afternoon, the woman came out on the deck. She stood and held onto the rail as if the wind might whip her out to sea. She stood that way for what seemed an eternity and then a younger woman—someone who was probably Anna's age—came out and took her by the arm. Anna's involvement in the scene was interrupted by Wayne's cries. There was a diaper to change, a baby to nurse, two children to bathe and dress and entertain.

"Mr. Vanderbilt left her," Anna said over a dinner of steamed shrimp, which the children would not eat, and french fries, which they would. "She's all alone. He ran off with his very young secretary and where does that leave her?" Anna was trying hard to make a joke of what she had seen but the humor was impossible to find.

"I think he died," Walter said, and she turned, her expression matching his. They both sat quietly, fries and catsup all over the plastic tablecloth that came with the house. "Yeah, he died all right," Walter said. "She's too peaceful for him not to be. If he'd just left her she'd be furious, breaking things, screaming for the lawyers. He died all right." It was a feeble joke, and though Anna laughed, she felt the tears spring to her eyes without warning. Summer after summer, they came to the same house, catching glimpses of the lady who came outside less and less; the Lincoln was no longer in the garage. With each passing summer, the children across the street got bigger and then they were doing things with Carol and Ben and Wayne. Carol reported that the house belonged to the kids' grandmother; there were twelve cousins in all. The children were still so young then: Ben down at the Putt-Putt range or pavilion playing pinball; Carol reading magazines with a girlfriend and talking about how no man was going to keep her from being an astronaut if that was what she decided to be; Wayne out riding the waves on a Styrofoam board. In her worst scenarios, tragedy came to them from beyond the boundaries and frames of their everyday lives: a car running a red light, an airplane engine dying, Ben drafted and dropped in a jungle, a stray bomb planted in a building where they happened to be visiting, a lunatic with a submachine gun in a fast-food chain. But instead it came from within, a heart that had never threatened anything except too much love, a fragile, easily broken organ.

*   *   *

"See you tonight, honey." That's the last thing Walter said, and she has spent countless times playing back through the phone conversation, imagining that unwitnessed day. Why didn't *she* feel something? Why didn't she, while singing songs of praises and drawing turkeys and pilgrim hats, get a sudden rush of goose flesh, a tightening in her own chest?

Now she steps up where a crowd has gathered in the center of the mall and is watching the closed curtains of a stage. People are pushing, up on tiptoe, to get a better look. *Welcome!* a big banner says and another says, *Eat to Win!* All of a sudden this little man in a white jumpsuit jumps from behind the curtain and bounces around, waving and circling his arms at his fans. It's the Exercise Man; she's seen him on TV before. People are lined up to catch a glimpse. She pulls her purse around in front of her and eases out of the crowd, goes down to the other end of the mall where there is a petting zoo. Young mothers are there with little ones who reach out and then shrink back from the hungry tongue of a billy goat.

"I worry about Wayne," he had said on the phone. It was early morning. She sat on the bed in her gown and robe, a cup of coffee on the nightstand. Out the window she could see the dogwood tree, leaves bright red, and down below, the school bus stopping for a crowd of children who filed up

the step and in through the narrow door, their arms filled
with lunchboxes and notebooks. She had a stack of construction paper on her dresser; the children would spend
the time during that day's lesson tracing their hands to
make turkey feathers. "I just don't think he seems satisfied."

"He will once he's taken that test," she told him. They
had visited Wayne once during law school at Columbia,
and he had spent the whole visit locked in his room "studying," though they'd heard him make many phone calls.
They had just gone ahead and ventured out as tourists,
seeing everything you can possibly see in Manhattan in
twenty-four hours. That night, after an early dinner, Wayne
went back to his studying, and they sat nursing their sore
feet and vowing how the next trip would last longer. They
had made the same promise just the year before when
she went with him to San Francisco. Walter had an early
meeting but then they rented a car and headed out. They
were determined to see everything from Alcatraz to China-
town, Walter singing like Tony Bennett every time they
saw a cable car. They had raced through downtown Seattle
the year before that. They loved the West Coast and had
always talked about taking another trip—a long relaxing
childless trip—as soon as Wayne passed the bar. *Son, I've
got to tell you*, Walter said the day they were leaving New
York, *I've never been able to pass a bar.*

"I hope that test is all that's bugging him," Water said

that morning on the phone. "He'll be home soon." That's when she looked at the clock and told him that she *had* to hurry, she was going to be late; somebody had to work.

"See you tonight, honey."

She thinks now that Walter was onto Wayne. He always seemed to *know* things. On Ben's first wedding day he said that he felt the marriage would never work; he just couldn't put his finger on it but something was wrong. *Carol will never go back to school if she marries this Trey fellow*, he had said. *This Trey fellow wants a woman in the house. I can tell. It may take a dozen children and shackles but he'll find a way.* Sometimes it makes her mad that he knew so damn much, was so perceptive about their children, could tell from her physical stance what mood she was in (uh-oh, the limp-wristed hand on the hip means depressed; straight wrist is mad as hell), but when it came time for him to know the most important moment, the danger that would rob him, her, all of them, he hadn't had a clue.

The first year was the hardest. Each day was an anniversary. Each day was a countdown of events. Nothing could pull her away from the timetable leading up to or away from his death. Her children tried. They took turns dumping the events of their lives at her feet, but she wouldn't be deflected. She got tired of listening to what was going on in *their* lives. She wanted her own life. Real or not, she wanted to be a part of something that was of her own design. She had to get out, go places, watch people. In her mind, she wrote long letters to the woman at the beach. *How could you just stand there?* she asked. *How could you be at peace?*

Now the third year is closing. Thanksgiving is around the corner. It's time to decide what kind of stuffing or dressing to prepare. But nothing equals a mall or an airport during the holidays. Both are bustling with people, and emotions are soaring. On the days she doesn't work, she alternates between the two. Carol says, "But *why* were you at the airport?" and Anna tells her that there are wonderful stores at the airport, that people shouldn't ask so many questions so close to the holidays. That was Walter's line. He had used it on the children from October 1st to December 25th, diverting their curiosities with hopes for a present. Her children want her to be the perfect widow, being led in and out of the house like the woman at the beach house. Anna imagines Mrs. Vanderbilt living out the rest of her life in silent composure as she yearns for those late afternoons with her husband (their dinners at Brady's Seafood) so long and so hard that she is stripped of all that was ever a part of her.

Children are so selfish the way they want to lead you around and keep your mind occupied with latch hooks or Phil Donahue. Carol says, *Why don't you get interested in a continuing program?* (Meaning a soap opera.) Trey disagrees with Carol's suggestion of *regular* programs. (He says he hopes she isn't watching such trash when he's out in the garage working!) He suggests Anna watch the Public Broadcasting System (*British* soap operas). Ben and Terri suggest she choose a craft (ivory-carving has done wonders for some people). Wayne says she'd be great at the soup kitchen, a breath of life for the down and out. *And who will give me a breath?* she asks.

Her children don't want her to talk about Walter anymore. They don't want her to talk about how he looked in the casket. She keeps saying, "He looked okay, but his mouth was wrong. Walter never held his mouth that way a day of his life."

"Really, Mother," Carol says and Anna wants to slap her, to shake her, to tell her *for godssakes get a divorce*. And Ben says, "Really, Mother," and she wants to ask how they can be so sympathetic with an alcoholic who murdered his family and not with a woman who had a wonderful happy marriage (complete with wonderful sex and happy private jokes) to a wonderful man and who wants to talk about it? Wayne says, "Really, Mother," and she wants to shake him, to ask how a son of hers and Walter's went such a route, holes in his ears and men on his arm. She wants to say, *Don't tell me what loneliness means. Don't you even try*. Dear God. Some nights she can't sleep because her mind flashes picture after picture, like slides. Walter. Wayne as an infant. Walter looking down at her, sheets twisted around their legs. Wayne running towards them with his suitcase, happy to leave summer camp, never to go again. Walter's eyes closing as he exhales, his heart beating rapidly, her hands on his back, pulling him toward her. Wayne in a shiny blue graduation gown. Walter's eyes closed as his heart beats rapidly, the telephone cord beyond his grasp, and Wayne with a male lover, sheets twisted around their legs. She shudders and cries out, unable to bear either picture.

She is at the airport at a gate that is crowded. Sunlight is streaming through the big glass windows. There is a man with a bouquet of flowers. A young girl wearing fatigue pants and a tight black T-shirt is slouched in a chair with her tote bag on the seat beside her. She's reading some kind of self-help book (*Making a Place for Yourself*) and will probably do so all the way to Dallas (it's clear from the boarding pass she clutches that she is leaving). Somewhere in this world (somewhere in Dallas/Fort Worth maybe) this girl has a place and there is someone waiting for her, her name running through that person's mind this very minute. The last time Anna was here she had witnessed a scene involving a lost child. The little girl's description was given over the loudspeaker time after time as the airport employee hugged her close and tried to get her to stop crying.

While the child sobbed, Anna had watched and wondered what Walter would have said when Wayne announced that he had a male lover? Alone, she had held her breath and counted long seconds, swallowed, focused. She said, "We," and then faltered with the plural, "we want you to be happy, Wayne. Nothing more." If Walter had been there, his large strong arm around her, she would not have been so understanding and sensitive. She would not have thought to remind herself how fragile it all is, fragile and precious. The lost child was red-faced. Her nose was running onto the stuffed toy she clutched. The airport employee looked at Anna and shook her head. "Can you believe this?" she asked. "Can you imagine a parent not keeping a better watch?"

"Oh God, there you are!" A woman rushed into the area, her face white and frantic, mascara ringing her eyes. "Oh, baby, baby." She grabbed the child and then turned to the airport employee. "My husband thought I had her," she was explaining, out of breath and needing to redeem herself. "I thought she was with him." The husband was there within seconds, a trail of suitcases strewn behind him as he wrapped his arms around the two. "Thank God," the man said.

Sometimes Anna imagines that she will turn in a crowded place and see him there, that they will reach each other with a babbling of how it was all a misunderstanding, that he didn't really die. "Oh, thank God," she sometimes wakes up saying, somehow confused that the dream where he was checking the air in her car tires is reality and the empty bed is not.

"See you tonight, honey," Walter says and hangs up the phone, turns to the simple moderately priced room. On the table by the window is his breakfast, orange juice and toast. He loves eggs and bacon but is watching his cholesterol. He quit smoking years ago. He walks at least a mile a day. He does everything just the way it's supposed to be done. In the closet is his blue suit, white shirt, red paisley tie. He has been traveling for years. The insurance business has been good for him, good for *them* financially. Retirement is just around the corner.

I left my heart in San Francisco. The third grade teacher thought it was an odd selection but couldn't help but smile at the chorus. They drew pictures, hearts like valentines riding up to the stars. "You can't leave your heart nowhere," a boy, still pink-faced from recess, said and grinned. "You'd die." He laughed, the whole class joining in. The teacher looked at Anna in a shocked worried way, which she brushed off with the wave of her hand. She thought of Mrs. Vanderbilt, her hands firm on the railing, her chin lifted as she stared out at the ocean.

"That's true," she said. "You would die without your heart."

"Oh, no." A girl at the front shook her head, her hand

up to her chest as if to check her own beating heart, while Anna attempted to explain *figurative*.

"What's a cable car?" Another child asked.

Now, people are filing through the jetway door, spilling into the hall with waves and shrieks. The man who has stood so quietly with the bouquet is moving forward, arms reaching for a young woman in blue jeans, her hair cropped in a thick blunt cut. "I thought I'd never get here," she says and kisses him full on the mouth, the flowers pressed between them. The girl in fatigues looks around as if annoyed by all the chatter and goes back to her book. Her flight can't board until all of these people have gotten off and the plane is tidied.

Anna thinks of the couple reunited with their lost child as if she knows them, as if they are distant relatives or old acquaintances. She imagines them at home, their house recently painted, a yard recently mowed, a bed with sheets just washed, their dinner thawing in the kitchen. They have gotten over what happened at the airport last week and have stopped studying each other with the unspoken, unintended accusation; but they still wake with a sudden rush of horror with all the things that *could* have happened that day. "You have such a morbid mind, sweetheart," Walter once said. The kids were at camp and she kept expecting a phone call: a broken arm, salmonella, stitches in the chin.

*   *   *

But *that* morning as she collected her construction paper and went to school, she had no such thoughts, no expectations of what was to come. She tries so hard to see it all. "See you tonight, honey," he says, and he hangs up the receiver. She imagines a hotel bedspread with matching striped draperies, art deco prints in chrome frames. He would have the draperies opened with the sunlight coming through. He would stand in front of the window and watch people coming and going on the street below. Maybe someone was watching him across the way. Maybe someone from another window in another building saw him turn suddenly. He felt sick and he turned to put down his coffee, but he didn't get there and he reached for the phone, their familiar number going through his mind like a secret message or song. Everywhere Anna looks, there is the message: life is fragile, so very very fragile. She watches the people exit, the crowd thinning temporarily before those departing make their way to the gate. Already the couple with the bouquet is at the end of the hallway, arms entwined as the flowers swing back and forth. Now the girl in the fatigues sits up straight, clutching her boarding pass.

"You going to Dallas?" the girl asks, and Anna is startled, turns quickly from the big glass window and shakes her head.

"Are you?"

"Yeah." The girl's voice is much higher than Anna would have expected, much younger. "Unfortunately."

"Oh." Anna waits for an explanation but the girl doesn't give it.

"I guess your person missed the flight," the girl says and points to the closed door.

"Yes." Anna feels the need to move now. To push herself down the hall and outside into the fresh autumn air. "I hope you have a good trip."

The girl smirks, runs a hand through her short stiff hair. "I won't. It's my dad. You know I *have* to go spend that weekend once every three months." She waits for Anna to nod and then goes back to her book.

Anna begins walking. By her next visit here, she will have constructed a setting for this girl where she will be happily reunited with her father. The father and girl will ask in amazement why they didn't see years ago how silly their problems were. They are parent and child—family. They will drive into Dallas and eat at a fine restaurant. Now Anna feels like a ghost, like someone haunting someone else's life, and so she concentrates on turkey and stuffing and her own children and grandchildren and school-children, and how she needs to construct or reconstruct her own scene. It's been exactly three years; now the fourth begins. There are details she will forget and need to reinvent in a simpler, gentler way. It will be a smoother progression, the nerves worn down. She passes gate after gate, each one identical.

If she could pick a time, they would load the station wagon and drive to the coast, the kids crowded in the back seat. It would be a long bright day—the children's squeals muffled by the roar of the surf—followed by a cool shower and a nap. And in the late afternoon as the children sat in a circle playing cards, as Walter still napped, she would cross the street and go stand by Mrs. Vanderbilt on the deck. She would take notes on loneliness (is it really possible to live with it?) and then rush back to her own bed to find Walter there, her love reaffirmed with his every breath.

Anna decides while walking the long hallway that she will not stuff her turkey. She will have a turkey breast; there will be a pan of dressing on the side. She will not have to put the heart, liver, and gizzard (those working parts) into her gravy because she won't have them in the first place. People are boarding at gate C-10. She will bake a chocolate cake so big and so rich that everyone will need to lie down right after dinner. They will nap and she will sit quietly on the patio, content to rest after a busy day, relieved to have some silence after all the talk, all the questions she has asked her children about their lives. There is a young woman in the hallway, her beige pumps a perfect match with her suit, diamond ring flashing on her smooth young hand. "See you tomorrow night," she calls and blows a kiss to the tall dark-haired man stepping into the boarding tunnel. He lifts a hand and is gone.

Comparison Shopping

The big news in my neighborhood is that Tom and Sue are going to be on "The Newlywed Game" or rather, "The *New* Newlywed Game," as Sue has corrected me over the past four months. It all started as a joke, a joke which, I might add, stems from my own little anecdote about what I had heard a woman answer one night while I was scanning my cable for something to watch. Bob Eubanks asked, "What vowel does your husband most resemble while asleep?" and the woman said, "*S*." Bob Eubanks said, "Oh, the *vowel S*," and the woman nodded. The next woman said a *T*, not a little *t* but a capital *T*, because her husband scrunched his shoulders up such that his arms were even with his head. Bob said, "Oh yes, the vowel *T*," and once again got an emphatic nod.

We were all sitting beside the subdivision pool when I

told that. Jack Crawford, who has too often been told that he bears a striking resemblance to Pat Sajak, and who had had too many drinks, laughed so hard that he fell into the pool, which prompted other people to follow. That's how it is here in Windhaven Estates; we all do the same things. Like if one person hangs out a flag just for the hell of it on some nondescript day, then by noon, all the flags are flying. I'm starting to get the hang of it all now, though it hasn't been easy.

Sue and I have been friends for years, one of those odd friendships where you have absolutely *nothing* in common and yet, for whatever reason, genuinely care about each other. We could not be more different, which is why I never would have imagined that I would one day begin imitating her life.

When we were in college, roommates by lottery, Sue was Halloween Queen and I was the editor of a small campus newspaper called ♀. Being Halloween Queen was a lot better than it sounds. It was a big deal if you were into the fraternity/sorority organizations; Sue's picture was plastered all over campus on a ballot with lots of other beauty queens, and every guy in every fraternity voted. She sat on the back of a convertible and rode down Main Street, smiling and waving and yelling, "Go Greek!," while guys whistled and made what I have always called catcalls. She wanted me to write an article about her and put her picture on the front of ♀, but I saw this story as a conflict of interests. Sue was the perfect example of what my newspaper was trying to destroy: she was coy and superficial and wore makeup every day of the week.

"Did you see me in the parade?" Sue asked as soon as she got back to our dorm room. She was standing there with an open bottle of champagne in one hand and a long-stemmed red rose in the other. It never occurred to her that I might be concentrating on something just because I was typing full blast. "Norlina? Yoo-hoo! Are you there?" She was using that little singsong voice of hers that seemed to charm every man on the face of the earth and just made me want to get sick. She hiked up her sequined evening dress and sat Indian style on her bed.

"No," I said and cut off my typewriter to emphasize that she had interrupted me. "I had too much work to do to go and stand on a corner and watch a parade."

"Well, pardon my ass." Sue traced her finger around the edge of her *Love Story* poster where Ali McGraw and Ryan O'Neil sat staring into our dorm room. "No, no. Let me take that back." She giggled and pulled her thick blond hair up on her head, then pointed to the little quote at the bottom of the poster. "Love means never having to say you're sorry."

"Sue," I said and gave her my most serious look, which wasn't difficult in those days given those thick ugly glasses I used to wear. "I am writing an article about how women need to be appreciated for more than their physical appearance." As soon as I heard myself say this I wished I hadn't. Sue had been trying to get me into contact lenses for over a year, and even with her head reeling from too much champagne, she took in my appearance from head to toe and burst out laughing.

"I'm not laughing *at* you, Norlina," she said, but then she didn't say anything else either, just told me to make sure she was up in an hour to get ready for her date, and then drifted off into a snoreless beautiful oblivion that I supposed came with having nothing else on your mind. It did, every now and then, enter my mind that I might be a touch bitter, seeing as how I had had one date my entire life, a blind date, which ended abruptly when the guy excused himself to a pay phone and came back to say that his grandfather just died and he had to go to Kansas.

"Kansas?" Sue asked when I returned early and interrupted the candlelight dinner she was serving on top of my desk to one of her many admirers, a little jar of red caviar opened and spilling on my only copy of my latest editorial. "He's not from Kansas."

"No," her date said. "And his only grandfather died last year."

"Oh," I said. As liberated and open-minded and realistic as you may be, there are those times when the sting of humiliation is unavoidable. And I felt it right then. I said something like, *Oh screw him, what a doofus he was anyway*, and I gathered up my work that had little red eggs clinging to it, and went off to a place where I often worked at night, the hall bathroom. It was not a bad place to work: the tile floor was cool on hot nights, the overhead lights were really bright; if you got thirsty or wanted to wash your face, there were fifteen sinks and fifteen mirrors. Whenever I was upset, I liked to write letters to Marabel Morgan and tell her how she was about as far from being a *Total Woman* as Clint Eastwood. *How can you be total without a brain, just tell me that? How can you stand to look at yourself in the mirror?* I was having trouble concentrating and so I went to look in the mirror at myself. I was about to splash my face (an easy thing to do if you don't wear makeup) and, just as I was leaning down, I caught a glimpse of Sue there in the doorway. She had a caviar cracker in one hand and a bottle of wine in the other.

"Norlina, Norlina, Norlina," she said and came and draped her arm around my neck, caviar cracker swinging near my eye. "It's not the end of the world."

"Did I say it was?" I stood up straight and stared at her. I was still in date attire, denim skirt and this prissy monogrammed T-shirt that Sue had given me for my birthday and insisted that I wear. I was wearing her lime green espadrilles, which matched the T-shirt. If I had let Sue, I would have had a big grosgrain bow in my hair; if I had listened to Sue, my hair would have been streaked ("It's such a drab color, Norlina") and permed ("It's lifeless and limp and too long and you have split ends").

"You don't have to say anything, Norlina," Sue said and

pressed her perfect little pink face next to mine. We looked like the before and after of a *Glamour* magazine makeover. "When you start writing to Marabel, I know what's up." She pointed to my legal pad in the corner where I had written *Marabel Morgan sucks eggs*, and shook her head. "C'mon." She pulled me by the arm, thrust that wine bottle in my hand and insisted that I turn it up. She didn't insist I drain it, but I did; I figured what the hell. "It's not the end of the world."

"Why do you keep saying that?" I squinted to get her in focus while I cleaned my glasses. "And where's the date?"

"I sent him on his way." Sue giggled and stuffed that cracker in her mouth. "I told him that you needed me more than he did."

"Gee, thanks," I said. "That was real smart." I imagined the guy now, back in some fraternity basement where the walls and windows were painted black. He'd be wondering so why was his date cut short? And answering himself, Well *because* Sue's poor pitiful ugly roommate got trashed by a guy who couldn't get dates either.

To be dumped is one thing, dumped by someone who is usually a dumpee, too, the very worst.

"I am smart, Norlina," Sue said as we moved down the long hall of the dormitory. "I am very very smart in many many ways." Whenever Sue drank, she started repeating herself. "You are prejudiced."

"Me?" I asked her. "I'm prejudiced?"

"About people like me and Marabelle," she said. "You are prejudiced against women who have a lot of sex."

"Yeah, right," I said, feeling mad because she was right, mad because *my* bed was all rumpled up where they had been making out, while Sue's bed looked like a picture out of some house-decorating book.

"What you need to know, Norlina," Sue said when the light was off and I was just about asleep, "is if you've got butter in your refrigerator, your man won't have to go getting some margarine on the street."

"What refrigerator?" I asked her. "What man?"

Occasionally Sue *has* been right and usually when I least expected it. I mean, who would have ever thought she was *right* when she suggested that I move into this neighborhood? It's taking time, to be sure, but I *am* adjusting. My first month here, I bought a color TV, VCR, cable hook-up, and a microwave. Money was no problem since I had saved a bundle living with Byron for those long seven years. *Down with Materialism and Up with Nature*. That was Byron's motto. He was a self-appointed forest ranger and we lived in a pup tent in the National Park. I had a job as the person who checks in campers and *did* get paid on a regular basis though Byron didn't even know it. He'd be off all day communing with nature and smoking dope. He'd say, "What did you do today, Norlina?" We'd be sitting there by the campfire, his pupils the size of Frisbees, and

I'd say that I had gone around and cleaned up after careless campers and had found some money and walked down to the Thriftway Grocery and bought the beans we were eating (I never told him they were originally *pork* and beans and I'd taken that scrap of meat and immediately eaten it). Now, I'm hooked on Lean Cuisines and Le Menus and I love every morsel. Now, I take a shower daily and I sell real estate and I only think of Byron when the crowd grills out at the Windhaven Estates Clubhouse.

"Where have you been, Norlina, that you don't even know how to work a microwave or a VCR?" Sue had asked me, laughing. For years, even though I stayed in touch with a postcard from time to time, somehow I had always avoided *really* telling Sue about my life with Byron, which I came to see later was in and of itself a sign that I was in the wrong place. I had missed Sue's wedding on account of Byron taking it upon himself for us to be on bear patrol. "You've got to help me, Norlina," he had said. "Ignorant visitors who feed them could get in big trouble." On Sue's wedding day, I was way up in a cedar tree waiting for somebody (like a real park ranger) to come and get us down and away from this particular spot where it seemed all the bears were hanging out.

Sue had not changed a bit, and I gave in to her just as if we were still there in the dormitory bathroom. First thing, I let her streak my hair with Clairol, and I let her make up my face and pick out some new clothes. I told my story, bending the truth a slight bit here and there, to save her the discomfort of a shock (I had outright lied to my mother, who thought I'd married an Egyptian archaeologist and returned with him to study the Great Pyramids).

I told Sue that I had married Byron (she met him in college) and that he'd become a forest ranger who did not believe in extravagant living. I did not let on, of course, that Byron was the one who married us because he believed there was no position that could not be self-appointed, or that we took vows to love and lust each other and never waste water or eat meat there near Buzzard's Gap.

"I really don't know why I married him," I told Sue, who was pulling my hair through little holes in a rubber cap with a crochet hook. (It hurts like hell to get your hair streaked, but I'm a true stoic, as hard and unbreakable as the piece of petrified wood that Byron gave me as a token of our union. "We will now exchange natural artifacts," he had said during our vows and pressed that wood into my palm. I gave him what he thought was an arrowhead but was really a man-made piece of costume jewelry I found in front of the freezer in Thriftway. I think it had been an earring before it got stepped on a lot.)

I told her I didn't know why I married Byron but really I do. Byron is the only man who ever showed me any interest, plain and simple. He walked up to me one clear blue day and asked me to sign a petition that said I wanted to boycott all restaurants that served meat. He stood there looking at me, ready to engage me in conversation just as soon as he had my signature. How could I resist *that*? Sometimes back then I'd measure time by how long I'd gone without another human speaking to me (except Sue of course, who had no choice but to talk to me since we lived together). It was like I was invisible the way that I could go for days without a human voice speaking directly to me as an individual. The longest I ever went was five days. That record was broken by somebody who knocked on my dorm door and said, "Do you have any liquor I can buy from you?" Of course I didn't, but I pretended I was looking while that tall thin guy stood there waiting. I wanted him to talk but all he said was, "Well, do you or don't you?" and when I shook my head, he turned and walked down to the next door. I heard the girl there (a friend of Sue's) say, *Why no, I don't care much for liquor myself unless of course I'm having a strawberry daiquiri. I really like the ones they make down at Barry's Bar, you know the place with the cover charge?* and he said, "Well, what are we waiting for?"

You can imagine then how good it made me feel to look up and have Byron standing right there in front of me and looking me right square—through the glasses—in the eye. Sure, I thought he looked a little strange with a big brand drawn on his bare back (red and black so it looked hot), fake blood all around his neck (like a slaughtered chicken), and two bricks tied to a rope and swinging from his waist right in front of the groin area (castration is unnatural!), but it had been so long since I'd *really* communicated with anyone. The readership of my paper had gotten so small I had had to fold, and I had been replaced by a magazine that kept the paper's name (adding the male genetic symbol). It was a billboard for personal ads, most of them with peculiar requests. "I can't believe your magazine!" Sue had said. "I mean, you go along with that stuff? All these variations on the theme of love?" No matter how many times I told her that it was *not* my magazine, she kept talking like it was. And she read that rag more than she had ever read anything in her life. "I don't get this at all," she must have said a thousand times a day. It was a dark dark time for sure.

And then, here was Byron, suited up for protest and holding out a ballpoint pen. I was the first person to sign, the first person he'd approached; he asked me to go sit with him in front of Burger King and ask customers how they would like to be hit in the head with a club, bled and carved, ground and charcoal broiled? One man said, "That's disgusting!" Byron just stared at the man in what I later came to think of as his *slack-jawed way*. It seemed his mouth was always sort of hanging open in a stupid gape and I should've taken note of that, should've known that it would eventually get to me.

*   *   *

I mean, all the signs were there; all the reasons why I shouldn't go live a self-appointed life in the woods with Byron, but I was desperate just to have a life. But still, with every little perfumed card I ever got from Sue, (I kept a post office box I went to once a month), with every daily trip down to the Thriftway Grocery (four miles down and four miles up), I started imagining myself in Sue's world, the thick rugs and carpet, the water beds and televisions and chlorinated pools. I imagined myself in a hot bubble bath and climbing between clean sheets and under a per-fumed comforter and the air-conditioning churning out all that manufactured coolness. The thoughts were certainly better than my reality: Byron hosing me down like a forest fire and then zipping me into that double sleeping bag that had God only knows what living down in the foot of it.

"What a cop-out," Byron said the day I packed my back-pack and headed down the trail. I can't tell you how pitiful he looked there in his torn faded jeans, his ribs showing like xylophone keys through that grungy white skin, those thin strands of cotton-candy hair pulled back and tied with that stringy old bandanna. It makes me itch to think of him and then it makes me laugh. It makes me laugh all the way into my kitchen, where I pop in a Le Menu, sweet and sour chicken, and watch its eleven-minute spin.

I laugh all the way over to my sectional sofa, from which I flip on my widescreen TV by remote. Any minute now

Tom and Sue will be on that screen right before my very eyes. Jack Crawford (who does look a little like Pat Sajak *would* if he had no hair and thirty extra pounds) is coming over to watch with me. He's no dream man but it's a lot better than being with Byron, and unlike Byron, who used to periodically take a vow of silence out of respect for the trees, Jack Crawford never shuts up. If I say the weather is nice, then Jack feels compelled to tell me *why*, (low humidity, the time of year, my house faces north, blah blah); if I say I don't care for black olives, he tells me why.

"You ought to be on 'Jeopardy,'" I said the night I'd just met him for the first time. "You know more than God." He smiled and thanked me while everybody got a good laugh, the intended sarcasm in my voice floating up and beyond all the strings of white minilights in the trees. So I thought why not relax and give these people a chance. Why not overlook the fact that these people aren't the smartest on the planet (and Byron was?). They do have good taste in belongings. I made a decision to work on my life, to try and fit in with these people. I mean, they are certainly more normal than Byron, and most importantly, they accept me as one of them.

I remember staring up at those little minilights (they would have sent Byron into a seizure) and thinking about it all. I remember thinking I could overlook the fact that Jack Crawford wore platform shoes and had bad breath.

(I mean, look at what I'd already lived through.) I could overlook that Sue's *perfect* man, Tom, had a vocabulary of about six words, most of them used twice and strung together to make statements like, "Oh, Sue Sue, you little cute cute." He *was* just as good-looking as she had always said and he did have an absolutely perfect body; so okay, give the man that. I decided right then and there to give it the benefit. After all, hadn't Sue gone out of her own little way to be there for me?

"Speaking of game shows," I had said and leaned forward. "The other night I was watching 'The Newlywed Game.' "

" 'The *New* Newlywed Game,' " Sue said and nodded to Tom, who was pinching up her little little cheek to kiss her cute cute self.

"Anyway, they asked this woman which vowel her husband most resembled while he slept. . . ." I continued my story, Jack Crawford staring a hole through my breasts. I was about to move quickly to startle him, to say something like *fill your eyes and then fill your pockets* but I just let it go. It had been a long time since anybody had looked at me. Next thing I knew, Jack sprang up like a jack-in-the-box and leapt into the pool fully clothed. Before too long we all followed.

"Let me explain to you why you want me," Jack said later, when the two of us were stretched out on my water-bed, his weight causing my side to buoy a good six inches higher.

"Do you have to?" I asked, and he said it was just what he was hoping, a woman who was all action and no talk; he'd read about such and whenever I was ready he could expound on the subject. He had heard that women like me, homely in the youthful years, sometimes suddenly blossomed like one of Georgia O'Keefe's sensuously sexy flowers, and would I like to hear what he knew about her or would I rather just go right ahead and *do my thing*?

Talk about a rock and a hard place. And *still* it was better than what I'd had there in the pup tent with Byron. It's sad sometimes how life is distorted by comparisons: good-better-best, when really you were never up to *good* at all. I just lay there and indulged my best fantasy to date, while Jack Crawford began going into what he called his *sexual trance* and which resembled some kind of dance like you might expect to see from a tribe of pygmies. My fantasy of the moment was this: I have married a handsome Indian doctor and live with him in Bombay, where he is a highly specialized surgeon revered by all. I wear saris and sandals and a veil over my face in public, but just let us get home and we go wild for each other, a trail of clothes strewn over my gleaming tile floors and expensive carpets. My liberal-minded sensitive surgeon sings and laughs the whole time he prepares dinner, while I put on The Rolling Stones and dance around in my underwear. We are incognito; we fit into society but we do not live by it. We eat lots of puff bread and curried rice and pork vindaloo; we eat crêpe suzettes and pasta primavera and Hostess Twinkies. This was the fantasy; and I closed my eyes tightly and brought to my mind sitar music, high twings and twangs, while Jack Crawford explained his rapid heartbeat and profuse sweating. It was quite a feat, but I could *still* maintain that life *could* be worse.

I have just finished my dinner when the doorbell rings and in strolls Jack with a box of Ritz crackers and a jar of peanut butter and an explanation about how he has found these foods to be aphrodisiacs for all the men in his family. "Oh," I say and tell him to sit down. The show is coming on right this second. Same music, same Bob Eubanks and there they are, Sue and Tom, all the way from Windhaven Estates.

"Everybody's watching," Jack whispers and reaches for my hand. Cracker crumbs are sticking to his damp palm. "I noticed while driving over. A television in every home. You know how there's a bluish-grayish glow in the window when a set is on. You know how it's like you're sitting in a room and turn a set off . . . ?" I have to blank my brain and comparison shop: Byron (scratching his head to see if any-thing has set up housekeeping there). Okay. Back to Jack. I can face him better now. Now I can also face Tom and Sue, who are doing real well. Sue has answered all of her ques-tions correctly: his favorite fast-food restaurant is Snoopy's Sushi; his former girlfriend's name is Trix; and he was most embarrassed the time Sue walked in and saw him trying on her underwear. "Yeah, I remember when that happened!" Jack says and kisses a mouthful of crumbs onto my cheek. "Yeah, that was when I was still with my ex, and we all got such a kick out of Sue's story that we all started wearing the spouse's undies, funny, huh?" I stare at Jack Crawford, fully expecting to see the slackest jaw of them all, a jaw so slack that it just swings back and forth like it's held by rubber bands, but, no sir, not Jack's jaw; it is moving up and down in tight mechanical bites, crackers spewing. All I can think about is *Jaws* and that multimillion-dollar machine they made to jump up and eat the boat and most of its inhabitants at the end.

Each time Tom has said, "Goody goody, Sue Sue," and now there's a commercial break, and now Sue is left to say what Tom will answer. Bob Eubanks is chuckling when they come back on. Sue obviously has said something *real* cute cute.

"Who will your husband say is your *strangest* friend?" Bob asks and goes down the line. I think Sue should say Kandi (she renamed herself), who heads up Welcome Wagon and has recently had both a breast enlargement and a fanny tuck. Jack thinks she should say him. "I mean, I *am* a little strange, you must admit," he keeps saying while all the other women tell their little stories. "I mean, how many men like me are still available? How many men who look like me are also interested in sexuality as is portrayed in both art and *National Geographic*?"

"I'll have to say my friend Norlina." Sue pronounces my name slowly.

"Hey, it's you." Jack leans forward and claps. "She said your name nice and slow so they can be sure and spell it right on the card."

I just sit back and wait, wondering what reasons she has. Is she going to say something about my past life? My life with Byron? I can't help but wonder if my mother is watching this. Maybe Tom and Sue had a deal. Maybe on the way to California, they figured up all these little patterns with set answers, like if Bob said his typical "My friend so-and-so is a real bow-wow," or "My friend so-and-so has the biggest bazookas," (something tacky and trashy like the way they always talk about "whoopee"), then Tom and Sue had decided to name me. If it had been a male friend, maybe it would have been Jack. After all, I've always thought that any couple with any sense could devise a system and easily win. That is, of course, if you want to win that year's supply of tomato soup and a recliner. I sit and *will* Bob Eubanks to move on to the next one, but he likes to linger with Sue. For the first time in this century Jack is quiet, and it is noticeable that he has bronchial problems.

"Why do you say she's strange?"

"Why not?" Sue asks and turns to the woman in the little cubicle beside her. What!? Has she forgotten that I'm here on the other side of the country and the other side of the tube? Does she think that a flight to California entitles her

to talk about me behind my back and to my face so that
Jack can hear about my pitiful wallflower type of youth,
which he will soon begin to *explain*? Even if they do mean
to win, enough is enough.

"I mean, well, there's just no way to explain Norlina.
She's been really weird since the first day I met her. I mean,
she looks weird, you know?" Sue lifts her hands as if to explain, her mouth all screwed up and off to one side as if in
imitation of *how I look.*

"Hey, that's pretty good," Jack says. "I've seen you do
that face before. It really requires quite a few of those facial
muscles, may be related to the set of your teeth. I know
every single dentist in town real well. I play golf with two
dentists often."

"I mean Norlina has *no taste*," Sue is saying. "Not even
in her mouth!" Bob Eubanks is holding his stomach. Sue is
really on a roll. "She used to live with a forest ranger and
before that she edited this magazine that got into all kinds
of weird sex. In college all she did was sit in the bathroom."

"Wait, wait," Bob says. "Let's hear about the weird sex."

"Like *really* weird," she whispers. "Like so weird I can't
even say."

"Hey hey hey," Jack says and gets a handful of Ritz. "I
want to know. I want to know." He puts his other arm
around me and jiggles. "You've been holding out on me,
firecracker."

"None of it is true," I say and move away from Jack, go

and put a cup of hot water in my microwave for a cup of coffee. I don't even want coffee, just to get away.

"They're back!" Jack screams, and I go in in time to hear Tom, who has never said more than six words, spout an encyclopedia's worth about me.

"Well, I know it's Norlina. Long before I met the woman, Sue had prepared me, you know. Like she'd make references to her weird roommate, Norlina, and so like finally one day, I said, 'So, Sue Sue, tell me about Norlina. *Why* is she so weird?'"

"Tom looks good on the tube, doesn't he?" Jack is sitting forward, shirt pulled up and pants hanging low enough around the belt to paint a most undesirable picture. "I think it's because he's got a big head. All the people who photo well on the tube have the big heads. Nancy Reagan, for starters. Think of all the stars."

Believe it or not, it is my desire that Jack keep talking.

"Yeah, Sue has always told me how at college she was afraid to sleep some nights."

"Afraid to sleep!?" I yell and push fat Jack off of me.

"Sue has always thought that Norlina had repressed sexual tendencies."

Where did he learn to talk all of a sudden? What, he's saved up a word a day his whole life to come on TV and douse me with public humiliation?

"You know. She's been fighting some kind of tendency ever since she was the editor of a small college newspaper that boasted many alternatives to sex, we're not sure what this tendency is, though, if it's lesbian or bi or, you know, nymphomania."

"We'll have to ask Jack," Sue shrieks and locks her arm through Tom's. She turns to Bob Eubanks and gestures with her other hand, palm upward like she's the little teapot. "You see, Norlina is dating a friend of ours." Come on now, Sue, I'm thinking. Let Jack have it, too.

"Great guy, Jack," Tom says and nods. "He's certainly one of the most intelligent of the kids we run with. Good old Jack, a man with a lot of valuable information."

"So maybe he's got the info on your friend," the woman in the next booth hoots, and they break for a commercial.

"Tom speaks well, doesn't he?" Jack is beaming now. His jaws are working in high gear. "But now I can't go for this double business, honey. If you've got a problem—you know, the first two things Tom mentioned—then you gotta let me in on it. I've got myself to think of." He crosses his leg toward the wall and locks his hands behind his neck. "I hate to think you've been using me."

"None of that is true," I say. "You've got to believe me." But Jack is acting as if I'm not even present and then I realize what I have been lowered to. I am begging a man to accept me; I am begging a man I can only tolerate by taking fantasy trips halfway around the world to accept me. I've done this before. With Byron I was the daughter of a real old and wise Chinaman whose young handsome apprentice communicated to me in poetic riddles. On his day off, he stopped with the poetry and we made passionate love in a sun-warmed marble pool, drank champagne, and made up dirty limericks while my father and the rest of the people supposed I was practicing my delivery of poetics. I wanted a dual life; I wanted to be accepted both outside and in. I wanted somebody who felt the same way.

"Thought a real man could cure you, didn't you?" Jack is saying, and I have to look at my world the way it really is; quickly, I have to comparison shop. My God, there *is* nothing worse!

Tom and Sue are center stage now; they are mounting their little his and her mopeds and waving at the TV cameras. I know that within twenty-four hours she will be at my front door explaining how they said all of that to be funny, how they just knew I'd get a big kick out of it. "Come ride the moped," she will say. "Come on, Norlina. It's not the end of the world." I want to pull her hair out by the roots and stuff it down the throat of her BIG MOUTH husband.

"Look," Jack finally says when Tom and Sue and their matching mopeds have been appropriately replaced by a commercial for Pepto-Bismol. "I mean, really." He wants me to say that I lust for his body, that I've got to have a hunk of real man. I'd rather eat the Great Wall of China, the Great Pyramid of Khufu, and the Taj Mahal, stone by stone, with my mother there to comment on how I'm going to ruin my teeth.

"I can't call you anymore," Fat Jack says. "Them's the breaks, toots. You tried and you lost. We can't all be a winner on 'Wheel of Fortune.' We can't all be Jack's 'spin.' " I close the door and try one more comparison shop: Children will stop in front of my house to stare. Cats with one eye and mange will make great pilgrimages to live in my part of the subdivision. I will feel humiliation and rage every time I hear Sue's moped putter by. But also, I will never fly another flag for no reason or sit in an overcrowded, pee-warm pool or sleep in the woods with a stoned-out-of-his-head man with poor hygiene and no words of wisdom. I will never mimic anyone else's likes and dislikes. I will stretch out on my water bed and be grateful that some Mr. Hefty doesn't make it rise and rock, be thankful that I don't have to conjure up a dish of pork vindaloo to explain to myself why my eyes are watering. I'll paint my Windhaven Estates house a lovely shade of pink, and I'll put up an eight-foot chain-link fence, plant sprigs of bamboo and kudzu on the borders of my neighbors' yards. I'll start an alternative paper, a little neighborhood rag for inquiring minds. I'll even invite my mother to come visit with her purse full of dental floss and Avon samples, and I'll show her the photos a stray camper took of me on my wedding day at Buzzard's Gap. I go into the bathroom and splash warm water on my face, study myself in the mirror. After so many wrong turns, after so many dead ends, it might seem I am right back where I started; but I know better. This time I'm starting out with a firm list of what I *don't* want in my life so that what I do want will be easier to find. I'm also starting out with every modern convenience and appliance known to woman and man. I feel for the first time that there is a place for me in this world and I no longer need a passport to get there.

Migration of the Love Bugs

My husband and I live in a tin can. He calls it *the streamline model*, the top of the line, the cream of the crop when it comes to moveable homes. *Ambulatory and proud of it.* That's Frank's motto and I guess it makes sense in a way, since he is the only one of six siblings who's still alive *and* walking, not to even mention that he spent his whole adult life setting things in concrete—house foundations and driveways, sidewalks that will remain until the New England winters crack them once too often and that new cement outfit that just opened comes in to redo the job.

We're in Florida now and the only concrete we own are the cinder blocks that keep our wheels from turning. "Can't we at least put our tin can up on a foundation like everybody else's?" I asked our first day here. "You know, pretend it's a real building rather than a souped-up vehicle?" He was in what he called his *retirement clothes*, pastel golfwear, though he has never touched a club. He was surveying the flat, swampy, treeless land as if this was the Exodus. Even that day, our belongings not even unpacked, I was thinking that if this was the Promised Land, Moses for sure dealt me a bad hand.

"I like knowing we can move at a moment's notice." He turned to me then, eyes wide. There was an exuberance about him that I found as foreign as the landscape. He didn't even look like my husband to me. He looked so small in those lightweight Easter-egg clothes. Where was the concrete dried gray on his knees? The bandanna in his back pocket? The heavy brogans I had decreed must always stay outside of our apartment door? "After all these years, Alice," he said and took my prize possession from my hands, my mother's silver tea service that I had carried on my lap all the way from Somerville, Massachusetts, "we're free to do anything we please." He kissed me quickly and then ceremoniously carried the silver service inside the tin can. I stood and watched this frail pastel imitation of my husband walk away with my only piece of inheritance and willed myself to wake up. I had never seen such an expansively bright sky, never felt such intense heat. I felt lightheaded, as if my whole world were encapsulated in some kind of vaporous bubble that could pop any given second. I closed my eyes tightly and waited.

"Alice!" Frank called. "Come see!" I opened my eyes, only to find the tin can in place, blinding me, and a swarm of sticky flies clinging to my pale arms. The Promised Land, Armageddon—who knew they'd be one and the same? "We've got a view of the driving range," Frank called in a voice so enthusiastic you might think he was Columbus and I was on board the Pinta. "I've for sure got to get some clubs, now."

There is no one in this neighborhood with naturally dark hair. The woman next door, her skin prunelike from what she refers to as her *southern upbringing* and what I (when alone with Frank) refer to as her *melodramatic melanoma-begging* life, has jet black hair that stains the fine teeth of the rattail comb that she uses to part and pincurl her hair. "I can't imagine living up there where you were," the woman says every time I see her. Her neck skin is like an accordian. *I can't imagine having hookworm*, I think but bite the words quickly. Frank claims every day that he has never been happier, and it makes me feel helplessly sad. It makes me question everything I've ever believed in.

"This is the life," he says after a round of golf lessons and a couple of martinis with the accordian's malnourished spouse. "You've got to give it a chance, Alice," he pleads. "The change is good for us." I want to tell him that I don't like change and never have and that he, the person who has bought me White Shoulders cologne every Christmas for years, should know that better than anyone. But instead, I tell him that I *am* giving it all a chance, that I am enjoying all this reading time that I never had before. Just this week I read an article about these very bugs that are driving me out of my mind, the ones that cling and stick to your skin whenever you walk outside. The article said that these bugs have created a boom in the market for car-headlight nets.

I'm not sure where the bugs started out, maybe in Canada, maybe on some cool lake in Maine, the White Mountains or the Green Mountains, or around the Cape. The article didn't discuss their origin, only that they are slowly migrating through Florida; their destination is always south of wherever they are. It's a very slow migration because their life story is so brief: hatch, have intercourse, produce, and die. It sounds like a normal enough life, except that these bugs only get one turn each at steps two and three. And since they're chronically on the move, no two steps happen in the same place; there's no time in their short, migrant lives for settling down.

When Carl was born, Frank stood outside the hospital nursery window for hours on end. Mothers were treated differently in those days; having a baby was like being sick, like having something removed surgically. We took a taxi, Frank's face turning stark white each time I gripped the front seat and bit my lip. "It'll be okay, it'll be okay," he kept saying, his hands and hair damp as we bumped along the icy streets. I passed out while staring into the pale gray eyes of a nurse and woke with a terrible headache, my whole world disoriented until I remembered where I was and what must have happened. Within minutes Frank was there just like in a scene from a movie, flowers and candy and a fuzzy stuffed bear. Suddenly there was a new picture, a new life, new plans of *some day*.

Imagine if Frank and I, like the bugs, had dropped dead at that moment. We would have missed everything that we have come to know as our life. Or maybe there wouldn't have even been a Carl because it took years for us to have him. The article didn't say what happened to the unsuccessful, the infertile bugs, if there is such an error of nature. You wonder. Do they get to try again or do they just go ahead and die under the false assumption that they were successful?

"Mom, are you okay?" Carl asked when I called to say we were where we were going, only bound by cinder blocks and a doormat that said welcome to the tin can. I could hear his wife, Anne, in the background. "Say hi to Nana and Pop," she was saying, and each time she spoke, we'd hear the small echo of Joseph, eighteen months old and miles and miles away. They live where Frank and I used to talk about living some day, in Brookline. It was something I never expected to *really* come about, just as I never really thought we'd end up here. There's a park across the street from their building with a rose garden and swings for the children. Just a little over a month ago we were sitting there, Frank going on and on about *here*, this place and how the weather would be so much better, so much healthier for both of us. I was already homesick just listening to him.

"Have you been home?" I asked Carl. "You know, by our building?" I felt like I needed to yell into the receiver. "I'm wondering if they ever fixed that broken windowpane in the front door?"

"Well, I haven't gotten out . . ."

"What do you mean, *our* building?" Frank asked. "Give me that phone." He laughed and took the receiver, Carl's voice trailing on about how it wasn't always convenient to just hop in the car or on the train and go. "Your mother is fine," he said and patted my arm. "Sure. Sure. She's going to love it once she gives it a chance." I caught a glimpse of us in the storm door, only to be alarmed by what I saw—a couple of dried-up sardines stuffed in a tin can.

I have to take a broom and sweep those sticky bugs off of our screens at least once a day. I read in the paper that they have been nicknamed the "love bugs" because that's all they get to do. It's a real mess since they're all just looking for a place to either procreate or die or possibly both. I can't help but think if the bugs *knew* what was going to happen, they'd choose a celibate life and potential longevity. Don't they have enough sense to look around and see what's happening, to witness the great fate? I sweep them to our cinder-block stoop and then into the hibiscus, a lush bush with flowers so fiery red I keep expecting it to speak to me. I feel disgust and I feel pity as I sweep the carnage, some of the carcasses still joined at the thorax. The article theorized that they are heading for Cuba. I can't imagine why they'd choose Cuba. I'm sure that when they arrive it'll be nothing like what they expected. Millions and zillions of bugs to have died in vain. If I were a love bug I'd have to stop midflight and ask just whose idea was this anyway?

We had rented our apartment in Somerville for forty years, and the rent was frozen for us, safe and stable. For years I watched others move in and then out; with each tenant exchange and new coat of paint the rent increased. I knew all the neighbors, smooth-faced college students or young families replacing people like ourselves who had either died or one day just packed up and left. I had strolled Carl up and down that street, waved to all the neighbors on porches and at windows. "You don't even know that many people anymore," Frank said just six months ago, and I explained that, no, I didn't know them like I had known various relatives and people who had been friends for forty years. But I recognized people; there were young people who looked up at *my* window and waved, a young woman next door who was always asking me what smelled so good in my kitchen. I knew that if we left, we could never afford to come back; the rent would skyrocket and what I had called home for forty years would be as unattainable as the moon.

The landlord already had the painters there in the hallway when I went in to look around one last time. There were clean white patches where Carl's picture had hung over the television set in our bedroom; there were bits of dried concrete in the corner of our closet where Frank threw his work clothes. There was an old ball of yarn that had belonged to our cat years before and had somehow fallen into a small space at the back of Carl's closet. Fitting, since it was in his closet that he had hidden the cat after sneaking it into the apartment. That was when he was only seven years old, and the cat slept in that same closet until Carl was a senior in high school. Finally the old cat went into the closet one Sunday afternoon and refused to come out. Carl was out at the movies with a girl in his class. Frank asked me to go down to the market and get him some bicarbonate, and while I was gone, he took the cat away so none of us would have to see it die.

I felt panic rise in my throat as I surveyed the apartment, pacing room to room and back. There was a mark on the living room ceiling made by a rocketing champagne cork on the day Carl and Anne got married. There were smudges on the kitchen doorframe where all of us held on while leaning into the living room to hear the conversation, or to announce dinner was almost ready. There was masking tape around one window pane in the bedroom, Frank's solution to the winter wind he had likened to a dog whistle. The painters were waiting. They would lay on a fresh coat of paint that would hide all traces of us. I excused myself a moment and then opened the window over the bathtub and leaned out onto the small flat section of roof where I had deserted a dying geranium. In the distance I could see the train, hear the familiar rumble as it made its way into the city, where it would spill all the people and scoop up some more. I thought of all those times I'd complained, my arms filled with shopping bags, while I stood and waited for the rush of wind that announced an approaching train. I wanted another chance; just one more trip into the city and I would return stoically, no complaint uttered.

My young neighbor, pregnant and cheerful, was watering her patio tomatoes. "We will miss you," she said, I assume speaking for her husband and unborn child, maybe for the whole building. I mouthed a thank-you and turned quickly, sat on the edge of the empty bathtub, my hand gripping the faucet. I grieved that I had never counted the baths taken there, never made little marks on the inside of the door with each passing day. I was sorry that I had not taken *longer* baths, that I had not simply lain back in my world and stared at the full green weeping willow which hid the building next door.

"Alice." Frank was there in the bathroom door, a young

wild-haired painter behind him. "I was getting worried." He turned then to the young man and said something about *women things*.

"You know that we can never come back," I told him, and he shook his head, hugged me close. "If we leave, we can't ever afford to come back."

"Sure we can, honey," he whispered. "But we won't *want* to. Wait and see."

Frank and I were both born right near where we lived all those years; we figure we walked the same streets, shopped in the same stores, saw all the same movies at the same time, but we never met until we were in our twenties. He had just come back from World War II and I was taking some business courses in night school. I went to a party at my cousin's house and there he was. He was already in the same concrete business where his father worked for years before him, and he was spending his day off setting my cousin's children's swingset in concrete. He was kneeling there, his big hands pouring cement, face flushed with the brisk March wind, his thick hair a deep auburn in the late afternoon light. "Once it dries, that swing is set for eternity," he told my cousin when he was all finished. "Won't budge an inch."

I tell Frank about the love bugs and he gets a good laugh, says that if I'm going to waste my time thinking about such, I might as well go ahead and join Ida, the accordian-

necked woman, at the bridge table. I do and by the end
of the afternoon, I have heard about every stage of her
daughter Catherine's life and everything about Catherine's
children and Catherine's Christmas Shoppe up in Georgia.
"You can buy yourself an ornament at any month of the
year," Ida says. "Walk inside of Catherine's shoppe, that's
shoppe with two *p*s and an *e*, mind you—sophisticated,
huh?—anyway, walk in there and you get a shiver like
it might be December and you're in a snowstorm, carols
playing, bells ringing." I stare at Ida's face, at her mouth
moving in a slow drawling way, her lipstick caked like clay
on her dry lips, and I long for winter, the hiss and whine of
a radiator, the rattling of ancient glass windows, windows
made long before anyone had heard the word *thermal*. I
wish it were Christmas in our apartment, and Frank had
just tiptoed in and slipped that bottle of White Shoulders
under the tree, leaned in the kitchen to say, *You'll never
guess what I just got for you.* I wish I were standing in
our neighborhood drugstore the first time I ever smelled
that fragrance. It was a drizzly autumn day, four-thirty
and already dark. I sprayed my wrists and then stepped out
onto the busy sidewalk, my umbrella raised as I walked
home, nothing on my mind other than the chicken I was
going to cook for dinner and the calculated minutes until
Frank got home. Carl was just an unnamed abstraction
that we had talked about for ten years; he was the child
we had finally accepted we'd never have.

  Ida is still talking, her voice like a buzz, while I see myself up on a chair, reaching to throw old wool blankets over the curtain rods to close out the whistling air, while Carl at ten months holds onto the coffee table and pulls himself up in a wobbly stance. I want to feel the sting of cold; to pull a wool hat down close around my face; to huddle into a seat on the train, Carl pulled close on my lap while we draw in warmth from the strangers collected there, alive to the flashing lights and popcorn smells, the surfacing to daylight and the cold gray sky, the river frozen like a sheet of glass, lights thrown in crazy patterns onto the trees in the Boston Common.

"Then you walk out and it's ninety-odd degrees, what do you think?" Ida asks. She is staring and I nod at her, returned suddenly to a much older body, a much quieter life, weather so eternally hot and humid that I feel like I might fly out and fling myself into the grille of a car. If I am going to sweat like a pig, then let me do it in Fenway Park or Filene's Basement. Let me have a purpose and a little dignity. "I said if there's something you want and can't find, Catherine could send it to you." Ida pauses and takes a sip of her fruity drink, some concoction I have refused. (It is always happy hour in the ambulatory senior citizens' park.)

"I like birds on my tree," Ida says. "Every year Catherine sends me a few new birds. You can't wait until December to get your ornaments. Any time of year is good. I want some woodpeckers, you know sort of a comical bird, for the grandbabies." I watch her neck, imagining strains of "Lady of Spain." All of a sudden I feel the hideous speckled nausea that comes just before fainting. I have to wipe my face with a tissue I dip in my ice water. I have to breathe deeply.

"My son and his family will be here," I finally tell her, though this is something we haven't decided for sure. Frank says we will not be making the long trip home, so we are hoping they'll come. Still, I know that if I were Anne and settled there in Brookline, her parents and siblings close by in New Hampshire, I would not drive to Hades to see any-body. "I have a simple tree, a biodegradable tree, popcorn, cranberries. I don't buy ornaments."

"Well." Ida is speechless for a fraction of a second. "Did I tell you about our son Harvey, the artist?"

"I still can't get over those bugs," I tell Frank late one night. Our bedroom is the width of the bed, and its ceiling curves with air vents. "I mean, what are they doing? Why don't they just stay put?" I know that he knows what I am insinuating but he just squeezes my hand.

"I know what's got you worried," he says, referring once again to what has *him* worried, hurricane season and what Carl calls *The Mobile Home Tornado Theory*. "First sign of a storm and we'll just move our cinder blocks aside and drive inland. There's nothing holding us down."

"Sounds easy enough," I say, knowing that he's describing what we've already done. Frank wasn't running *to* this new place as much as he was running *away* from our old one. *First sign of a storm* (or old age—legs that can't make the apartment stair climb, bones too brittle to risk icy sidewalks) *and we'll just move.* It makes me ache to picture our home at night, the familiar shapes and shadows of our belongings. Maybe Frank had a similar vision at one time, a picture of one of us sitting there alone, nothing to break the silence but the distant hum of a passing train. Maybe he felt the unknown survivor should begin letting go by degrees, throwing off old treasured relics that would only become burdens when the other one was gone. He knew, for example, that I would never stare out at this golf course and see any bits of our past. He would never look at the cheap flip-down table and be reminded of my elaborate holiday dinners. He didn't take time to see that the memories would be there all the same, that they might even be heightened by the strangeness of an unfamiliar place. I suppose he thought when one of us died the other could simply move away from the grief. His plan of action was as simple as taking a dying house cat from its home. Or maybe he didn't see any of these things; maybe an instinct to run had come to him out of nature without realization or explanation.

"As for the bugs," he says, "what's foolish is that they don't stop and stay right here for a while, in the lap of luxury." He says the word *luxury* with a slight shake of his head, as if in awe, this impossible dream that he has convinced himself just came true.

"They have a terribly short life," I say.

"Yeah, and the men bugs have really got it bad." He rolls into me, his hand on my hip. In the faint glow from the streetlight in front of Ida's double-wide, he almost looks the way I remember from the first time we met; it was the same day he poured concrete around the legs of the swingset in my cousin's yard, a cluster of children watching. "The men bugs only have three stages of life. At least the women get that extra one."

"Birth? That's the bonus?" I ask. "You're saying you'd like to give birth."

"Well, can't be much to laying a little egg."

"Try a seven-pound-and-ten-ounce egg, try that," I say, and then he pulls me close and I try to imagine us in our bedroom with the full-size window and lace panel curtains; the window overlooks a sidewalk that Frank's daddy poured not long before the market on the corner opened. The market has fresh fruits and vegetables that the clerks arrange on tables out on the sidewalk; even in the rain, you can stand under the bright green awnings and fill your bag. Carl is a baby napping in a crib; he is a teenager sprawled in front of the TV set with that cat stretched out on his chest. I close my eyes when I feel like crying but Frank doesn't notice; he jiggles me and laughs, pulls me closer, and I imagine Carl in his small apartment, Anne beside him. I imagine them halfway listening to each other, halfway listening for the baby's cry, and, once again, the bathtub drained, another night unnumbered. Maybe they are too tired to hold each other, too tired to tell about the day, to say our neighbor said this to me or you'll never believe who I bumped into when I went into the city or when I was on the train. They tell themselves that some day they won't be so tired.

When I returned home from getting Frank his bicarbonate that Sunday afternoon, he was staring out the window, the cat nowhere in sight. I went to the kitchen to put away the things I had bought, noticing immediately that the cat food was gone, the bowls, the rubber mouse. There was a quietness as we sat and waited to hear Carl coming up the stairs. "I just didn't think it was right," Frank finally said when the three of us were sitting there. "House cats are deprived of nature." Carl shrugged, lowered his head to hide any response. "It's just a cat," he finally said and left the room.

Frank is snoring quietly now, his warm arm draped over my stomach. I want to wake him, to tell him that there's no such thing as paradise; there is no Promised Land. At journey's end, it is all a mirage, a picture of the journey itself and all we left behind. Wherever we are, here or inland or a hundred miles south, that's all that there is. There is nothing that can make the end easier for whoever is left behind. That's what I want to tell him but I don't. He is sleeping so peacefully, so satisfied with the accomplishments of his life; yet, even as he sleeps, he is preparing for some day when at a moment's notice one of us must take flight.

Waiting for Hard Times to End

I haven't heard from my sister, Rhonda, in over a week now, and I'm starting to get worried. My boss at Thriftway Grocery, which is where I work after school, tells me there's no reason for me to worry, that he bets Rhonda has better things to do than to sit and write out a card to me. "I know what kind that Rhonda is," he said and laughed. I don't like the way he laughs or the way his bushy eyebrows go up when he talks about Rhonda. "You know what kind Rhonda is, now don't you, Bunny?" he asked, and I just shook my head and went back to counting up the cans of B&M Baked Beans.

I'm tired of being called Bunny, but nobody in this town is going to change and call me by my right name, which is Saralyn. I've never minded that Rhonda called me Bunny because she made it up years ago because of the way my teeth look and because she said I always look scared and on the verge of bolting off. I do feel scared sometimes but I'm not always sure why. I'd be a whole lot less scared if I'd just hear from Rhonda. She left home two years ago when I was just fourteen and I have missed her ever since. We had some times, me and Rhonda. She used to make up my eyes and take me down to Ho Jo's, where she was the hostess. "This is my baby sister," she would tell people, and I'd sit up straight on my stool and nod at the person. "She's the sweetest," Rhonda would say about me, and it made me feel so good. Sometimes Rhonda would buy me dinner, and we'd sit at one of the tables and let somebody wait on us. The man who ran Ho Jo's would always want to sit with us and Rhonda would say, "Another time, Bill," then wink, so she didn't hurt his feelings. "This is mine and Bunny's night." Then when it started getting late, she'd put me in a taxi. "I don't want somebody trying to pick you up. Tell Mother I'll be home later after I'm through work-ing," she would say, and I would, and my mother would get red in the face and shake her head, mad that I had on blue eyeshadow and only thirteen. "Don't you be like her," Mama said.

I haven't seen Rhonda in two years, but almost every single day I have gotten a postcard. I'm the only person in my family that keeps up with Rhonda; nobody else wants to hear what she has to say. Sometimes I get scared that they might not give me my card, so that's why I'm always there when the mailman comes and why I did not go to 4-H camp last year when everybody wanted me to. They wanted me to, mainly because I had sewed the best dress and they thought I'd win our group a prize. I sew pretty dresses, all right, but they don't look good on me because of my shape; I don't have a shape. I have made Rhonda a pink silky party dress, which I'm saving for when she comes home.

I love the cards that she sends; no two have ever been the same. I guess that's why I hate holidays so much— because the mail doesn't come. The only other times that Rhonda has not written to me have been during what she calls "hard times." When I spread all my cards on the bed-room floor, I can see that there have been quite a few hard times but never one that lasted over a week. They'll start back real soon now. The first card to come after a hard time always says, "WHEW!" I'm expecting to get one of those any day now. Rhonda will say WHEW! and tell me what happened.

The first card I ever got was two days after she left home. She had promised she would send one; she had hugged me so tight and told me that she would always keep in touch. "You are what makes it all bearable for me, Bunny," she had said. "You know that I love you the most?" I nodded and then she was gone and I did like she said. I didn't tell anybody that I had seen her; I didn't tell that she came by the Thriftway and had gotten herself a ride out of town with a man in a pickup. "There's a man in South Carolina that I need to see," she had told me. "He's in love with me and I need to decide what I'm going to do." She told me that I'd see one day that having a man in your life changes a lot of things. "But no man will ever change how I feel for you." I stood in front of Thriftway and waved until I couldn't see her blond hair flying out the window, couldn't see which way the truck had gone.

The first card—a giant size—has a picture of the Honeymoon Bed in the Honeymoon Suite of Pedro's Motel down in South of the Border, South Carolina. It is a beautiful bed with a rich-looking pink satin spread and little pillows, mirrors all around. I have never been to South of the Border, but I've heard of it, heard of fireworks and putt-putt ranges and gift shops and restaurants. I could've gone with the 4-H group last summer, but I passed because they were going to Myrtle Beach and I would've missed the mail for three days. Rhonda isn't there anymore. When I first got this card I kept thinking about how wonderful it would be if I was there, how wonderful it would be if I was sitting on a stool right there near Rhonda while she introduced me to people.

Hey Bunny! I'm Mrs. Elwood Smith, now. We have been married one hour. I hate you aren't here with me. You know you're my maid of honor and if I had known I was getting married, I would have bought you a beautiful dress (and grown-up hose and high heels!) and had you here with me. But sometimes things just happen real fast. (You will know what I mean soon enough.) Just remember, you haven't lost a sister but gained a brother! (And you will like him better than Ned. HA!) I'm gonna live down here of course. I'll miss you but don't you worry! You'll be on a bus and visiting real soon. Elwood is in the shower. (Weddings make him sweat, he says. HA!) He is a card. You will love him like he will love you. Please tell Mama and Ho Jo's that I won't be back! Thanx 10,000 pesos! R

Nobody was happy for Rhonda and Elwood Smith like I was. Mama and my brothers, Ned and Billy, just frowned and shook their heads. Ned and Billy are both older than Rhonda and they're married. They married the Townsend sisters, who Rhonda always calls "The Gruesome Two- some." "She'll be back," I heard Mama tell Ned and Billy. "She don't have a pot to pee in."

"Well, well, well," that man at Ho Jo's said. "Wonder what it's costing little Rhonda Sue to live down there?"

The second card gave me all the answers, but nobody even wanted to hear about it. The Townsend sisters took me to buy some clothes, said I shouldn't be wearing Rhonda's hand-me-downs. I tried to tell them it was okay. She wrote real tiny on this card to fit it all on:

Bunny! Little Bunny! All of the clothes I left in my closet are for you! Elwood bought me a whole new wardrobe. See the dress Lady Di is wearing on the front of this card? Well, I have a black one *just* like it. Elwood doesn't look like Charles, though, thank God. HA! He has little ears, looks more like Al Pacino, you know? I hope one day you find someone like him and can move to a nice place like where we live. I go to the beach near about every day. I have a wonderful tan. I'll look into bus schedules to see when you can come. Elwood's paying so don't work too hard at the Thriftway and *don't* let any boys do to you what I told you they might try! Take it easy baby, *Rhonda*

Mama and the Townsends cleaned out Rhonda's closet and threw everything away. "She'll deserve that if she thinks she can show her face here again," Mama said, and I took Rhonda's blue-jean jacket with the diamond-looking things sewn in and hid it. I don't know why she didn't take that with her except maybe she wanted me to have it.

I can shuffle Rhonda's cards up and read 'em like tiny stories, or I can put them all in the right order and read them like a real long letter. That's what I do at night when Mama's watching TV. Right now I feel like shuffling and trying to remember where each one fits in the big piece.

Hard times, Bunny. Forgive me for not writing. Enjoy being a little girl (you know what I mean) because being grown ain't all nylon hose and eyeshadow. The little girl on this card made me think of you. It made me cry. Look at her digging in the sand with her little

pail. She is at Myrtle Beach and soon you will be, too.
I want to wait until Elwood comes home, though. Stick
your tongue out at the Gruesome Twosome for me and
tell Mama, "Smile. Can't crack your face more than it's
cracked!" Just kidding. HA! Love, *Rhonda*

Happy Birthday! Sweet fifteen. I wish I could be there.
I bought you a beautiful present but am going to save
it for when you come. You keep asking *when* and all I
know is that it depends on my job. I am moving right up
in this world, work long hard hours. When you come,
I can take off. I know what I was doing at fifteen and I
hope you know what you're doing! Got a fella? I bet you
do! I bet you look like the front of this card. I bet you
don't even look like Bunny anymore! Buddy says, "Blow
hard!" (He means the candles of course.) I'll call you
this weekend when it's cheap. *Rhonda*

I turn that card over and stare at the picture of Marilyn
Monroe, bent over, her hands keeping that dress from blowing all the way up. Boy, Rhonda couldn't really think I'd
ever look like that, but Rhonda kind of looks like it, boobs
and all. I had planned to tell her that but she didn't call that
weekend. Buddy had been in a wreck, she wrote me later.
He got twenty stitches in his head. "Is she still with that
man?" Mama asked me once, and I just said, "No." I didn't
tell her how Elwood had taken all the money that she had
saved and left. I didn't tell how Rhonda had herself a job as

a restaurant manager and was making so much money she didn't know what to do with it except travel. She traveled all over the country, all the places you'd ever want to see. One of my favorite cards is of the Grand Canyon and it is beautiful. It says, "It'll take your breath away!"

Didn't take my breath! Still breathing, still smoking, too. HA! You're going to love this place, Bunny. I'm thinking I might settle here. I'll fly you out, OK? It's sweet what you said in your letter (before Elwood robbed me!) about how you've made me a gift. Just wait until you see all the gifts I have for you! They fill up one whole room of the condo I'm staying in. It'll be like Christmas when we get together. I'm glad you like that boy—what's his name?—in your 4-H group. Let him know you like him, you know? Take my advice. They will be lined up for you real soon like they are for me here. Whoops! There's Bronco (a nickname) right now. Love, *R*

I still don't like to think about the time I got that card. It's been over a year now, but I've never been able to look at Rudy Thompson since. I waited for him after the 4-H meeting. I remember it all like it's a movie or a postcard. I was wearing Rhonda's blue-jean jacket, and I had on some hoop earrings and some lipstick that I had put on in the bathroom right after our meeting. I had just been told that I had the best piece of sewing, and Rudy had gotten a blue ribbon for his pet pig. "Hi, there," I said when Rudy came out. I tried to say it the way Rhonda would; I let my eyes droop a little like Rhonda used to do to that man at Ho Jo's when she wanted the night off. "I need to talk to you," I whispered, because that's what Rhonda on the New Mexico postcard had suggested. "He'll have to step closer," she had written. "So wear some cologne so you don't smell like Thriftway."

"Yeah?" Rudy stepped closer, and I felt my heart beating so fast when he did. "What is it?" He has green green eyes and kind of rusty-looking hair. He was wearing a belt buckle that had a big bull on it.

"I like your belt buckle," I whispered and closed my eyes, leaned back against a tree like Rhonda would do. "It's sexy." That was the part I practiced the longest. Rhonda had said it always worked for her.

"What?" Rudy acted like he was frozen, and it made me have to stand up straight, to smear that lipstick off a little with the back of my hand. "Bunny?" he asked, making the most horrible face, like he'd been expecting Coca-Cola and got buttermilk. Then they were all there, everybody, listening in, Rudy's face so red I thought he might kill me. "Sexy?" a boy called out. "Wooo wooo, Rudy!" All the girls were just staring at me like I might have been green and I wished I was green. I wished I was dead, but more than anything, I wished I was with Rhonda in one of those fancy motels where she likes to go, places with big bathtubs for a bubble bath and champagne, though Rhonda says I have to wait a little longer, maybe a year, before champagne. I ran home as fast as I could; that word, *sexy*, sounded in my head over and over like the principal at school on the P. A. system or like what Rhonda had described when she was in that bar that got raided that time. Rhonda said the police had done that, called everybody out, took everybody to the police station, and made them spend the night. *And there I was just minding my own business*, she had written. *What ignorant pigs! They made me take my clothes off! HA! I know why, too—a cheap thrill for the deprived slobs who work there.*

I have never been able to look Rudy in the eye since. It has taken a whole year for people to stop teasing me. I'd be in the cafeteria line and I'd hear somebody say, "It's so sexy." Sometimes Rhonda doesn't stay in one place long enough to get my cards, but she did get the one that told what happened. She wrote me right back, too. She sent a card that she must have saved from South of the Border way back because it had a picture of that giant-size Mexican Pedro which I still have not seen. The 4-H people who can talk to me without laughing told me that you can see that giant Pedro for miles. Anyway, now I don't even have to see it for real because I've got the picture:

Bunny. I'm sorry that what's-his-name didn't bite the hook. They don't always, you know? Why I had a man break up with me just last week. (Of course, I had threatened to tell his wife. I hear that's what Marilyn Monroe did to the Kennedy boys so I figured what the hell?) DON'T mess with married ones. They are *never* right in the head. That should just let you know that what's-his-name is *dumb* like most of the men in that town. I hate your boss. Did I ever tell you? He tried to get me to you-know-what once and I was insulted. If he ever makes up bad things about me, that's why. I'll be so glad when you can move and be with me. Then you'll meet some nice people. Love, R

One of the funniest cards has Mona Lisa on the front and Rhonda had written: "Well, I see Mama is *trying* to smile." And then another has a cartoon of a two-headed martian and the martian is disagreeing with himself. One head says, "I want to go out," and the other head says, "I want to stay home." Below it is printed, "Ever have trouble making up your mind? Two heads are not better than one." Rhonda had written: "I see the Townsends haven't changed a bit! HA!" Of course, I would never show any of these cards. I keep hoping that when I move and live with Rhonda, Mama and Ned and Billy will start to be nice to her.

Another funny card has a picture of this dog peeing on a tobacco plant and it says, "Have your cigarettes been tasting funny?" Rhonda had written, "You better not be smoking. If you do, you will love it and never ever stop. Jim and I go through five packs a day." When I got that one I smoked one cigarette. I didn't like it, but it had made me feel kind of grown-up and close to Rhonda. It was just last summer that I smoked it. I took one out of my boss's pack, and then I sat out back of Thriftway on an orange crate and smoked it. It was kind of nice in a way because I could hear people talking inside and hear the big freezer humming, Willie Nelson on the radio, but I felt real safe. "You can always count on me, Bunny," Rhonda had just written on a beautiful silver valentine card.

But now I'm looking for those cards that came right after hard times, so maybe I can figure out what's keeping Rhonda so long from writing this time. There's the one after Elwood robbed her, the one after she had to take her clothes off and stay in the jail, and here's another one. It's from the Statue of Liberty in New York City. Rhonda had circled the blond head of a woman that's in the crowd looking, and from the back it really does look like her. "That's me!" she had written and then on the back:

Hey Bunny! Whew! I have finally seen the light. (Get it?) I've had hard times, have decided men aren't worth the trouble. You'll see. All they want is to get in your pants or steal your money. Don't fall for the tricks. I've been trashed too many times but now I'm starting over: good job/new friends. By the time you graduate (and you do need that diploma), I'll be ready for you to move in. Right now I'm staying with a friend who says I really should be an actress! Imagine!! This city has

everything! I have a whole new life. I don't eat meat.
Love and Liberty, *Rhonda*

I love the New York cards the best. They are so funny
and happy. The pictures have all these bridges and lights
and the Empire State building, places you only hear about.
But there are still other hard-time cards. I had gone a week
without hearing from her, and then I got this one that has
people at Niagara Falls. The water is so beautiful, falling
there; there's a rainbow in the spray, and people are just
standing there in yellow raincoats like the Safety Patrol
people wear, standing so close to the little fence there before it drops off. I love the picture and I remember how
glad I was to see it after having waited so long.

This is not a honeymoon so don't even think it!
Randy (he's a good friend) came with me. I don't know
what I would have done that last week in New York
without him! He saved me. That's why I haven't written. Hard Times, but thanks to Randy, I'm okay. He is
such a card, looks real "sexy" in his yellow raincoat.
How are you? Knocking the boys dead? I bet you are . . .
more later. Love, *R*

After Randy ran off without a word, after she had taken
care of him, *practically supported him* for six months, there
was another lapse. That's why I was so worried at the
sophomore dance. I don't know if I would've had a good

time anyway; I went with Sandy Scott, who has teeth bigger than mine and a neck like a giraffe. I wasn't going to go at all, but Rhonda always told me that I should go places "because you never know who you'll meet. You can go on a date. It doesn't mean you have to *marry* him! My God, I'd have been married a hundred times by now!" Sandy Scott asked me to dance one time, and the rest of the night we just sat at our table and watched other people. He folded his napkin in and out like an accordian and told me about his daddy's heifer who had won a prize at the state fair. I guess he had heard what everybody else had heard, that I had liked Rudy that time. Everybody knew that Rudy's daddy *always* has prize hogs and cows. Rudy was out on the floor slow-dancing, and it made me feel funny inside to watch him; I guess I felt funny because of all that Rhonda had told me about what men will try to do, and because I hadn't heard from her. When I finally did hear, she was back down in South Carolina and had gotten a job in a Myrtle Beach bar. *It's a long way from Ho Jo's*, she had said and I was so relieved. When Sandy Scott called and asked me to go see *Return of the Jedi*, I went, but I didn't meet anybody else and I didn't have a very good time.

I think that Rhonda has probably moved again and not had time to write, or maybe she's been suntanning, or going to that amusement park she's told me about. I close my eyes and try to imagine all of the pictures in my mind before going to sleep. I see Rhonda and a handsome man riding the Ferris wheel, while I stand on the ground and look up at them, a huge teddy bear in my arms that a boy like Rudy has won for me over at the shooting range. Rhonda waves her hand, her yellow hair flying in the wind every time they hit the top, and me and that boy wave back, all of us happy to be there together down in Myrtle Beach. I hear my door crack open and I know my mama's standing there like she does every night. She's checking to make sure I'm in my bed and have not run off like Rhonda. "She's like a prison guard," Rhonda told me years ago. "She will never get over the fact that she couldn't hold on to Daddy." I don't remember my daddy at all; I only know what Rhonda has told me, that he was good-looking and full of life and it would have killed him to stay there. "She's not going to keep me either," Rhonda had said. "And don't you worry, Bunny. I'll come rescue you one day." Now I hear Mama shuffling down the hall, and it makes me wish that things were different for all of us. Sometimes I feel like I don't understand Mama at all.

"Did he touch you?" she had asked when I got home from the dance. I shook my head and then she was crying and holding onto me. "I'm sorry," she kept saying, but I'm not sure for what. Maybe because Rhonda was gone.

It's been two weeks now since I've heard from Rhonda. I'm sitting out back on my orange crate and my boss doesn't even care. He's been asking about Rhonda lately, asking in

a way where he doesn't laugh and his eyebrows don't go
that funny way. "Where do you guess she is?" he asked just
before I came out here. I told him I bet she has a new job
in a new city, or maybe she's run off and gotten married. I
hear the bell at the front of the store ring so I know I need
to be getting back in so I can ring the person up. I'm just
ready for the day to be over so I can get home and check
the mail. I bet it'll be there, some funny message about the
Townsend girls or Mama smiling.

"Hey," I hear, but I can't see through the wire mesh
of the screen door to know who it is. Before I can ask,
Rudy Thompson steps out here and leans against the building where somebody has spray-painted GO TO HELL in lopsided letters. "Haven't seen you at 4-H lately," he says. "Or
school." That's true, because I haven't been in three days—
been going down to Sikes Pond and sitting instead. "You
been sick?"

"What's it to you?" I ask, remembering that that's what
Rhonda had said to a man one time. Rhonda said, "That
silenced the jerk!" I must have done it wrong because Rudy
just shrugs and his face turns pink. Now I don't know what
to say, so I just wave a stick in the dirt and wait for him
to leave. *They will always leave you. One minute he's there
and the next minute he's gone.* How did he know I wasn't
at school?

"I was just hoping you weren't sick." He steps forward
and puts his shoe up on the orange crate; his foot is so

close, I could retie his shoe if I wanted. *Oh yeah, they love you when they can get something. In your pants and in your wallet.* I shake my head and, for the first time in a year, I look Rudy Thompson in the face. *You got to learn to stare them down. Get the upper hand.* His eyes are just as green as before, as green as that Atlantic Ocean; Myrtle Beach, South Carolina; The Grand Strand. Where is she? "I've been wanting to talk to you," he says and looks away. "You remember that time—" I know what he's going to say and I don't even want to hear it.

"No, I don't remember," I tell him before he can finish. *Sometimes I play dumb for Elwood because he thinks it's cute. HA!*

"Well, I wanted to tell you I was sorry that I didn't stick up for you," he says. "I just didn't know what to say. I mean, you looked so grown-up that day and all, and I had never seen you look like that." *Wear my blue-jean jacket and make up your eyes like I told you. That'll get him! I bet one of these days you look just like me, Little Bunny! (Hope you don't mind. HA!)*

I see the mailman's truck go by and I know his routine so well; he'll be at my house in fifteen minutes. "I gotta go," I say, and standing, I take off my Thriftway apron.

"I wanted to ask you to go to the movies," he says, and I don't have time to think. I have fourteen minutes to check out with my boss and run home. "I've been wanting to ask you but—"

"I gotta go," I say. "Really, I have to go." I open the screen door, my mind on Rhonda and the card. If my mama gets it, it'll be gone.

"Will you think about it?" he asks, his forehead wrinkling, and I nod, once again looking at those clear green eyes. *Keep 'em guessing.* I have twelve minutes. "Can I call you?"

"Yes," I say and run through the store, the buzz of the freezer so loud, my steps so loud.

"Hey, what's the hurry?" my boss asks. He looks to the back of the store where Rudy is standing and still looking confused. Shaking his head, my boss laughs like he knows everything, but I don't take the time to hear what he's gotta say. I throw down my apron and I am gone, running so fast down the street, the sun low and gold behind the big tree branches. Rudy Thompson's face keeps popping in my mind, but I don't have time to think about it right now. *Sometimes people will ask you out just to use you.* I turn the corner just in time to see the mail truck stop in front of my house. I run faster and pretend I don't see Mama out there on the front porch. She is walking down the sidewalk, but I get there first and reach my hand in.

"I need to talk to you, Saralyn," Mama says, and I wait for her to turn around so I can see if there's a card for me. "Why are you so eager for the mail?" she has asked before, and I always come up with one reason or another. I haven't shown or told her about a card in months now, but

I know she knows. I know because every time Rhonda's name comes up, which isn't real often, they all look at me like I know something. They have tricked me a few times by saying things like, "I bet Rhonda is in Canada," only to have me slip and give the real answer. I have quit talking.

"There's no card from her," Mama says, and I turn slowly, so angry. "Rhonda has gotten herself killed."

I wait a long time before I go inside; I wait until it's dark and the light there in the living room comes on. When I get inside the doorway, I hear the policeman saying they got no traces, that Rhonda was there in the Sleepy Pelican Motel somewhere near Georgia. I listen while he tells all about it: it looked like there had been a struggle, looked like they had been drinking. Shot there in the heart. I don't want to even get a picture in my mind.

Nobody at school has said a thing about Rhonda to me. My boss just said he was sorry, real sorry. "Let it be a lesson, Saralyn," my mama said, and I wanted to be called Bunny so bad I thought I'd die. I went to the movies with Rudy Thompson and afterwards we went and sat down near the pond. He didn't ask me about Rhonda but I knew he wanted to know. *They will use you to get what they want. I can't wait for you to get out of that hole.* I kept hearing Rhonda talking to me the whole time that Rudy and I sat there. He held my hand and it made me feel so funny all over, like maybe I was doing something wrong. He asked me why I never went on the school trips or club trips out of town, and I said because I didn't want to go anywhere, didn't need to go anywhere. "I know what it all looks like," I told him, and then I saw the real pictures, the motel room where they said she had lived, the way they found her without any clothes at all. It made me feel cold all over and I told Rudy I had to go home. I told Rudy if he was after me to use me up that he better forget it. "I like you, Bunny," he said, and I wanted so bad to believe him.

Rudy still calls me; he called just this morning to ask me if I wanted to ride down to South Carolina with him and his mama and daddy. "We're going to the beach for the weekend," he said. "You can tell your mama that my whole family's going." I imagined me and Rudy on that Ferris wheel, the stuffed bear, putt-putt ranges. But it was all too close.

"I've got to work," I told him. "But how about we go to the show when you get back?" Rudy paused like he was disappointed, but then he said he thought he knew why I didn't want to go down there. He said he wanted to go with me, steady, just me, and I said all right.

Now I'm in my checkout and Henry (my boss) is sitting over on the counter. He's been real sweet to me lately, told me that he was sorry for things that he had said about Rhonda, said he used to really like her and that she wouldn't have anything to do with him. "I would have done her right," he said, and part of me believed that.

"So, what's new with you, Bunny?" he asks, leaning back against the wall.

"Going steady with Rudy Thompson," I say. It's the first time I've said it outside the house. My sisters-in-law thought it was worth a Chinese dinner in Clemmonsville. My mama said she'd like for him to come by real soon.

"Well, well," Henry says and laughs. "I thought you'd looked different these days, all fixed up and smiling."

"Yeah," I say. *Having a man in your life will change a lot of things.* I look away from Henry to the street where the mail truck is passing right now. I feel myself ready to run from the store. Sometimes I keep thinking that I will get home and reach in that box and it will be there. "Whew!" it will say, and there will be pictures of all the places she's been. I still feel that way and sometimes I wonder if I always will. Sometimes I think I'd just rather stay right here and get the pictures of all those places, the lights and the bridges. And then all of a sudden I will see the other picture, the real picture that never did and never will be on a postcard, that motel room, that night. *No man will ever change how I feel about you.* I wish I could tell her she was wrong. I wait for the mail truck to move out of my sight, and then I tell Henry to call me Saralyn. "That's my real name," I say.

Words Gone Bad

I don't believe in nonviolence. I never have. That's what I tell my co-worker, Bennie, when we take our break and meet out on the wall that faces the University's clock tower. Bennie and I have been arguing over the world for years. We see it all from opposite ends. He says black and I say white. He says hot and I say cold. The only thing we agree about is that we like each other just fine and would be hard pressed to name an older or better friend. Bennie says, "The future is there for our people, Mary." He says, "Bend a little," though I rarely do. He says that for such a skinny dried-up black woman, I sure have got a mouth. I tell him, yes, and for a black man he's done all right. I tell him that if he wasn't married and we were thirty years younger (and if I was interested in any such thing), I might go for him.

Bennie went to all the meetings back during the marches. I can remember seeing the man, so much younger then, straight and tall as he led the way. He locked arms with others and swayed from side to side as he come down Richmond Avenue singing "We Shall Overcome," and I hung onto a porch post and turned my face away from them so I could take in the voices and remember it by sound alone, sweet words in the air. I didn't want to see any face of impatience made by somebody in a car having to stop and wait as the parade went forth. We could show him impatience. I didn't want to see nothing sailing through the air towards a soul marching there. I didn't want to hear some cheap crossness coming out from behind my own front door where I probably had a man (there were quite a few in my younger foolish days) that I wished I'd never seen laid up on the couch. I listened to the marchers' voices long after they'd passed. I felt uplifted by the *ideas* and *beliefs* behind it all. I felt like a part of a whole—a small link in a long rusty chain—and whenever I caught myself feeling like a woman all alone in the world with the responsibility of six children to raise, I conjured the strength of those words back to my ear.

Bennie said years after that he remembered seeing me there with my head turned to the wind and that his wife, Paulette, had prayed for me. He said all him and Paulette had heard of me then was that I ran wild, as wild as those black-eyed Susans that have taken over where my parents are laid down. They heard I'd been in this town since the day I was born and that I knew everything and everybody worth knowing and then some. He said Paulette had toyed with the notion of asking me to church; we got a laugh over that, all right. I told Bennie that the saints would have fell from the sky if I'd darkened a door, that's how long it's been. I hadn't been to a church since my first baby was born dead. It seemed like all those other children were just me trying to bring that child back again one more time. In my mind I called him Lazarus; in real life I called the man I was with (not the daddy) Lazy Ass. The daddy was a fine man, somebody I always believed meant well, except for the fact that he was already married. All those men, all those babies, I was looking for what I'd lost. But I don't go on about none of that with Bennie.

I said, I was wild, that's right. I'd go out to Buzzy's place on a Saturday night and drink white liquor like a man. If I sat down at a table with my sister Rosa and our aunt Libby, when we rose up to go there was a lot of liquor gone. We were women who could drink like mad, and when the sun rose on a Sunday morning and it was time to come on out of the club, we were among the standing. I've known a lot of men who needed to be carried. I've had several along the way that did. But I have never in my life had to be carried in no way. That's what I told Bennie when we first met and that's been years ago. I said, I'll shoot myself through the head before I get scooped up and carried off.

Bennie said he didn't believe in such, couldn't cotton to
any kind of violence, or to that kind of drinking and taking
up with bed partners. Bennie believes in God Almighty and
the afterlife; he believes we're all the same color when our
train pulls in.

I said, Smell the coffee, Bennie. If there's a heaven it'll
probably be split up in all kind of crazy ways just like a
piece of real estate. I was sitting out on my porch not a
year ago and a woman come by all ready to talk, all ready
to tell me about a life of peace and how it can be mine. I
said, And how much does this cost, this peace, or is it a
piece, a piece of candy or watermelon or strawberry pie?
(To this day I will not stoop to have some man at the gro-
cer's grin when I buy a piece of melon, and I'll drop dead
before I have it). The woman took out her little pamphlets
and handed them to me, and I gave her the eye (Bennie
always laughs when I show my mean bad evil eye). She
said they were free, all I had to do was be ready for her
to come back in two days to tell me some more about this
peace I'm missing.

"Price is too high." I handed her back her papers and
watched her mouth go tight while she clamped them back
in her bag. She was as black as me and I didn't care. I knew
when I saw her standing there in the middle of the road
with a little suitcase like the *big* folks carry that she was
up to no good. No sir, makes no difference to me if you're
white, black, or green come poaching me. "Go read your

Bible," I told her, and she backed a step like I'd slapped her. "The Bible will tell you that you're gonna be crying for some peace—yes, screeching your heart out for some peace—but it ain't here. No." I shook my head and stood up from my chair. To be so skinny, I'm a tall woman, and I pulled myself up straight and looked down on her smooth-combed hair. I started to ask her why she was working so hard to straighten and plaster down her *God-given* hair, but I had other fish to fry. "It ain't on this earth," I said. "The peace just ain't here." She turned and walked down my sidewalk and then collected there in the street with her other club members, each with a handful of those little books. They stared over at me and I gave the eye, then I started laughing; I laughed till I had to sit back down and put my head on my knees. Bennie got a good laugh about it all, but it was no time before he got to feeling like he needed to work on my soul a little bit, soften me up or something.

I told him then, and I'm still telling him, that I don't believe in nonviolence but I'm all for those who do; I'm proud of what results have been good. I'm all for their peaceful marches and protests if they are for a fact peaceful, peaceful like lilies on a Easter Sunday, like a white rosebud on a child's chest to boast love for a mama gone by the by. I'm for peaceful lilies and still waters, brother-hood and firm handshakes, prayers whispered in the head, but I've seen something described as peaceful only to then see it was as peaceful as a hog butchering, as peaceful as a fire hose turned loose like a big wild snake down a city street. I've seen dark peaceful nights, a baby on my lap in a peaceful sleep only to have it woke by a nasty voice telling me what I've been doing wrong, woke by the sound of a dark heavy fist busting up a warped washstand mirror and leaving it there for my broom to come around tomorrow; I saw the men come and go, every time with the going me hoping I'd never see that face coming my way again, though I did keep hoping there would be *another* face. Somehow I kept hoping there was love and happiness in my forecast; it took hurricanes and tornadoes and tidal waves and a little of everything else to convince me otherwise. Bennie said I was watching the wrong weather report, and I said I can't believe there was ever good weather for a woman like me. I've seen spray-painted bricks red as blood, scrawled-out letters like a child might make, only a child don't spell those words so easy and a child can't get hisself up there to do it. Anger, words of hate, lopsided and crazy. Words of peace, about peace to peace. Give peace a chance, they might write, and somebody puts *fuck you* beneath it.

My office at the university is in the basement, a long windowless hall lit up at each end by the humming red Coke machines. My door is at the end there by the stairs, where the feet echo loud and clear all through the morning, a rustle of bookbags and the jingle of pocket change, the cold slap of that canned Coke rolling down, the whoosh and fizz as the can is opened. Feet scurry back up to class where there are big wood-framed windows that stay open near about the whole year, in summer when the heat of day and those clustered young bodies is too much to bear and in winter when the old radiators hiss and whine uncontrollably as they breathe the heat. They sit there, some professor slouched on a wooden desk, leg carelessly swung over the desk top, lectern set crooked on the floor. Some want a lectern and some don't. Some leave notes that might say *Please do not move the lectern*, like they are all that remain on earth.

They ball up papers in nervous palms and pick those little confetti pieces from rough-edged paper ripped out of a notebook to snow down onto the floor; brush it away, brush it away, and there's always words on the board, words and words and more words in their dusty slanted lines of white and yellow, erasers filled with words gone old or bad or both, used up day before yesterday and some not even in English. Their words carry over my head, their accents so foreign to this part of the world. They speak French and German and who knows what else, and these professors come and go, some in little old caps cocked off to one side like it might be good for something. What? Ain't no warmth in such a hat, no different from placing a crocheted poodle over a roll of toilet paper, no purpose but adornment, putting on an appearance. I know a woman who has spent her *life* crocheting toilet-roll poodles and for what? I once asked her for what. I know she isn't earning her keep, isn't setting any table with those fit for the bathroom dogs. She sells them for less than the cost of the yarn to people with bad taste who lean out of their car windows and toss her some coins. "But maybe she's happy, Mary," Bennie said to me one day and put me in my place for a while. SPEAK ENGLISH, I'm always wanting to say when those students pass me by, sidestepping a neat little pile of sweepings, those long black spooky overcoats they like to wear breezing my pile of work away.

Their words sound peaceful sometimes, these nothing sounds that come to my ears, but then you look those sounds up in a dictionary or a textbook that might be left there on a windowsill or kicked down the hallway and you find there's nothing peaceful about *afflige*; nothing peaceful about *mal de mer* or *pomme de terre*. All that for a potato. I want to stick my head in the doorway and say, *Mange* your *pomme de terre* then and pick up your droppings when you leave the room.

Peaceful is something you imagine when you close your eyes at night. It's those times that you remember so good as being the very best times you know: being a child with a sack of penny candy that you count out on an old quilt, or thinking you've fallen for a good good man. I think of my babies, all of them forty years old or better and living in places like D.C., where they got good jobs and drive good cars. No Greyhound waiting for my children. From the time they could follow my words at all I was saying don't let your life go for waste, nobody's going to pick up your mess but you. I took my youngest son to get hisself a used car so he could drive back and forth to school, and that white man standing there asked us, well, who would be paying for this car, and I pulled a roll of bills from my purse and I stepped up close to him, oh yes, so close he could see I meant business, so close I smelled his old cheap cologne, and I said I mean to give you a down payment today and then make payments from then on until my son here gets his job. These hands didn't get this way from watching the TV, I said, and held my palms up to him. I did not blink until it was all done and signed. I didn't take my eyes off of his slick fingers. Peaceful is what you feel *after* you've acted. They say *calm before a storm* but no, I can't believe in that. You may not see that turbulence, you may not hear the thunder but it's there all the same. Peaceful is reserved for after the action, after you've done what you had to do. Peaceful is something you tell yourself you will feel one day when it is all over and you've found a better home.

The students write their words on pieces of paper and the fronts of their notebooks. They write them on the walls above the urinals, and then I scrub them off letter by letter, and though they might add some little bit of spouting from a textbook, some fancy long-winded words holding it all together, their words is no different from those in the bus station or in a rat-ridden alley. I put cleanser on a rag and I wipe their fucks and damns and shits, their *educated* words.

Not too many weeks ago I saw a young girl, her tam cocked to the side of her head as she listened to a young man speaking of his goings ons, his little summer vacation ABROAD; and she nodded her pretty little head, with a smile frozen there because she'd been no such place. She listened while he tossed down some paper scraps, and her eyes cut over at me, her eyes as dark as mine, her face and hands, and there was a second when she recognized me, somebody she knows, and a part of her wanted to slap his abroad-gone hand and tell him you know better than to toss trash to a clean floor, but she couldn't do it and when she felt me looking, she turned away ashamed and ignorant of what to do or what to feel. Don't you see my office, this closet, don't you see this sign taped here for anybody who's buying himself a Coca-Cola to read and know what I do? Clean the bathrooms. Clean what's on the wall. Get up all the paper scraps and dust those erasers. I have a thought that the walls into heaven are littered with ignorant bits of orders. I have to believe that or else I couldn't do a thing. I'm working towards peace but there's no peaceful way to do it. I wanted to grab that young lady by her thin shoulders and shake till her teeth rattled; I wanted to say if you was my child, girl, you would have some serious explaining about how you can stand here and talk to this French-speaking white dishrag-looking boy while I am watching and waiting to stoop down and clean his droppings.

"I roomed with an African-American guy," that boy said, shifted his books so some more bits of litter snowed on my floor. "You may know him." But when the name was called, my little weak putting-on-airs love shook her head no, instead of saying what I was wanting to hear, which was: And so I suspect you must know the president of the University, you must know Dr. Robert Conway Taylor, who is a white man like yourself. "Momma, you do over-react," my girl, Denise, has said in the past, usually when I've got one of the grandbabies on my lap and I'm telling him how he's always gotta be ready to jump in the ring; and I say yes, maybe I do, but there's reason, there's good solid reason why I do. I'm angry. I don't deny that I'm a mad woman sometimes, and I can give you a list as long as my skinny leg to tell you why. And yes I like that sound; I like to hear *African-American* the same way my great-grandmother liked hearing *emancipation*, but there is more to it than *the words*. In all of life there is more to it than the word; words can get washed off and thrown out, but just show me what does those words mean to you, what kind of act is coming with those words. Those words might sound so pretty but are they? When I was carrying my oldest baby that lived (I was just sixteen), I heard somebody say something of the fontanel, and I thought what a beautiful word that was, soft like a feather on the wind, and then come to find out that word was my darkest fear, that word was that tender pulsing soft spot that let me know she was living, that place you had to worry over and care for so gently, her little mind so vulnerable until the bones had grown and cemented there. Over my head I hear *fromage*, *fromage*, and we have had some laughs over all that, me and Bennie, nothing but cheese. He might hand me out a slice of American cheese his old lady packed with some light bread and he say, Oh Mary, shall we eat this here fromage? A kick. Yes Lord, I *like* the sound of *African-American*, but I've been called so much you better be ready to give me more than two words.

Bennie spends most of his time in the administrative building, where he's got a bright fluorescent-lit office. We find books left on the windowsills and in the trash cans, have for years, and we share them out like a library. I told my children years ago that they better never go destroying property that way, if they were going to destroy something then find something that needs destroying. You find it and then I'll be there to help you; yes sir, you get me riled up and any riot you've every heard of will look like a little dog fight.

"Oh now, don't you worry over that paper you dropped," I said to that dishrag boy, all the while looking at that pretty young girl, those eyes all aglow with high hopes of

African-American equality brought directly to her on the wings of this washed-out big-talking boy. "No, honey, just as soon as you go on to class, I'll be able to catch my breath and stoop there to *retrieve* it."

"Oh, did I drop that?" he asked, his eyes wide as he smiled what he thought was a sweet look and what I thought was a putdown.

"Yes, you did." I said with a nod, and then I waited, the girl glancing down the hall where that window was open at the end; every pane in that old window was sparkling, and beyond it there was a blue southern sky and a chilly October wind, two things that are shared by all. The girl smiled at me when the boy knelt down and collected his droppings; she wanted to let me know that he *was* a nice boy, that he did respect her and me both just as if we were his own. I gave my head a quick shake and turned away to hide my laugh. I can use that psychology stuff too.

"This is what they all learn," I told Bennie one day and showed him one of their textbooks. "All these students get just enough of this stuff to put bad ideas into action."

"And maybe some good ideas," Bennie added. Lord, he is a good pure man. He believes in peace and he believes in nonviolence; he believes he will see it on this earth and he has still not given up on trying to get me to agree with him. "People mean well, Mary," he said. "Look at how far we've come."

"And still a long way to go."

"But the way come has got to mean something." Bennie was sitting there eating the leftovers his old lady had packed up in Saran Wrap. Paulette works in women's homes, ironing and cleaning and watching Oprah Winfrey when she can. Paulette is just as good and peaceful as Bennie, and I marvel and have for years at this miracle of two such good people finding each other when the odds is so stacked against it. That was the day I told him that if I'd've found a black man like him rather than all those I'd had, I wouldn't all the time be needing to ride my broom and talk so strong and ugly. "But how many men are in your league, Bennie?"

"Don't go putting down my gender," he said. "You'll make me mad, girl." I had to laugh, just the thought of Bennie all fuming was something to imagine. I got to laughing and then had to tell him what I'd seen on one of those talk shows, this fella who is trying to prove out all the differences between the white man and the black man. This fella was saying how whites are smarter and how blacks have more sex. He was saying how all those talks about black men's equipment is right. I said, WHAT? and I near about jumped into my TV set, near about mounted my broom and flew in. I said, How do you know? You going around door to door and pulling everybody's pants down? You going to crack skulls and measure the minds there? I know I don't speak lots of languages. I speak English and sometimes that isn't great but I speak the language of truth. I learned that language at the school of hard knocks. I went to school on my broom.

"Rode with your eyes closed," Bennie added and laughed. "If they come to my house I'll say that I ain't about to pull my pants down until I've gotten Mary's opinion and permission."

Every now and then I need to test him. Every now and then we read just enough in one of those cast-off books to get something going. Old foolish things like if a tree falls in the forest or if you close the door is the chair still there. Bennie said, "If it ain't, somebody did some fast moving," and we laughed until we near about split, students eyeing us like we'd gone off the end. "Clean has to be complete, I think," I told him one day. "If you've got a speck of dirt then you've got dirt and it's not clean anymore."

"So you just keep right on working," he said. "And bit by bit it gets cleaned up."

"I don't know if it's possible," I told him. "Dirty can stay dirty without anybody's help but clean can't stay clean."

"I can't follow you today, Mary," he said. "I give." He waved his handkerchief like a surrender flag, then mopped his forehead and crammed it back in his pocket. "But I do believe in hard work," he added quietly. "I believe it pays off in the end."

"I know you do," I said. "But you also believe in three on a match and that you ought not wash on New Year's Day. You won't go near a ladder that's propped up against a wall." He laughed, but then he got that quiet solemn look on his face, the look that says, *I believe, I believe.*

Bennie looks that same way when he hands me a slip of paper with his name on it that tells him to come and get hisself retired. Just like that, all his years are gone. Just like that, he opens up some fancy letter that says, "Get Out."

"Retirement, girl," he says. "It's just retirement. It's what we all wait for, what we work for."

"There's a catch," I say. "It's no different than some child with a dollar bill taped to a string to jerk out of some poor old fool's hand."

"It's all in print, woman," he says. "They're going to pay me to set at home. I earned it and I'm going to get it. You will too in another few years. It's good, Mary. It's good."

"It's not so easy," I say and level my eyes. "They want you out, probably got some old white fella all lined up and ready to slip into your place. I wouldn't spend that money too soon, no sir, it'll get snatched sure as you think it's there."

"Mary, Mary." He puts his hands on my shoulders and squeezes. In all these years of working together this is the closest we've ever stood. I can smell the detergent of his shirt and I get a sudden picture of Paulette in some cozy kitchen with her iron pressing out his sleeves and collar. I envy her that place and all that I've missed by not finding somebody like Bennie for my own. If I was the woman I used to be, I'd grab the man and kiss him full on the mouth right now. I'd be telling myself, *Oh yes, I can have this one if I want him, I can lay the fool flat,* but now I just want to stand here and look at him. "It ain't black or white or rich or poor or—" He pauses and then laughs and shakes me. "Or fat or skinny. It's just got to do with age, baby. That's all."

"You're sure?" I whisper and look away across what is known as the quad, where the leaves are flying in a tornado swirl of orange. I don't want him to see my weakness; I know I'm there at the crack—the *chink* in my armor suit, they say. When Bennie goes his own way, I'll be left with nothing at all. Except for a weekend phone call from one of my children or some crazy come knocking on my door to sell me brooms or Peace, Bennie is who I talk to. Bennie is who I look forward to seeing. Sometimes, if I weren't so well seasoned with the bad weather, I'd think I might love him.

"Believe me, Mary." His hand lifts my chin and we look at each other. "You believe, don't you?" I nod, trying to think of something smart-ass to say when he gives me that dose of *God loves you, Mary*. I'll say, well, then why don't he send me some candy and roses. "I'm going to miss you, Mary," Bennie says. "As tough a bird as you are. As ornery and mule-headed." He waits for me to laugh. "I sure will miss you." He opens his mouth to give me a little more of this sob song, this long goodbye, but I tell him to go the hell on and get his old mess of a watch. I tell him I hope it'll keep time better than he tells a joke. I start to ask him why he waited until the last minute to tell me but I guess I know the answer. I wouldn't have taken it well. I imagine that he's been thinking about it for months now, him and Paulette planning out their twilight time in the evenings after he's listened to me fuss on the rapes and the murders and the almighty white man.

Sometimes, like now as I watch him move through the leaves, the wind blowing cool and not a cloud in the sky, I even think I might *believe* something, just as I did as a child with a white rosebud on my chest, my mother's sister from out of town singing "Love Lifted Me" in a clear deep voice. I felt a peaceful stirring then, much like I did with Bennie touching me. But I find it hard to believe that there's room for peace in a world where people have to live in fear for their lives. Peace is in another world, the product of a nicer place. I'll defend my right to walk on this earth. I'll do my best to make sure I walk just as smooth as I can. If you slap me, then you just better brace yourself to get it right back. No sir, if you pick a fight with me, I'll do what I have to do to put it to an end. I don't start any fighting but I sure will finish one off, and when I go to bed at night I owe nobody nothing and Jesus himself would be ashamed to turn on me with a look of disgust. If you throw a tomato at my back, I'll turn around and cram it down your damn throat. If you throw a piece of trash to the ground then I'll do my damnedest to make you feel like a worthless pig. And all the while I'll hold my head way up high because maybe, just maybe, I *am* on my way to something. Maybe I might have to wait for another world to see it, and maybe I might have to read all sorts of trashy words written along the way, but just maybe there *is* something peaceful waiting on me, something more than a word. I watch Bennie make his way up the long stone steps at the end of the quad, the sunlight circling his path, and I imagine that Paulette cannot wait to hear him at their front door. She can't wait to tell him that she is so proud, that she truly does believe. Because of him, she believes.

Sleeping Beauty, Revised

It's late fall and my refrigerator is covered in autumn leaves ironed between pieces of wax paper. Every day Jeffrey brings something home from preschool, a treasure to be hung on the wall or around my neck, like the food-colored pasta necklace he presented me with today. On a Post-it alongside a bright yellow maple leaf is the name of the man I'm meeting for dinner—Phil, who is in computer sales, a friend of a friend, the first date I've had since I married Nick, which means the first date I've had in nine years.

"He's getting a divorce, too," my friend Sarah, who teaches with me in the junior high school, had said. Sarah is known for her matchmaking attempts, quick to seize any common variables that two people might have. "Three out of ten setups have resulted in marriage," she said.

What? You have two legs, a nose, and a mother? So does he!

Now I've done everything except remove the hot rollers from my hair when our babysitter, a bubbling pepster of a girl, calls to tell me that she can't come after all, that she dislocated her elbow while doing a back handspring in gymnastics class.

"I have an ice pack," I say and then recognize the desperation in my voice. I force a laugh. The girl is repeating what I just said to her mother. "Of course I'm kidding," I say loudly when I hear her mother voicing shock. "You tell your mother I was just kidding."

Our other sitter (also a high school senior) is at a *Cola Hour* being given in her honor. I know because I declined the invitation with the excuse of a *previous engagement* (I was still having trouble saying, "I have a date"). The party was being given by a circle of well-meaning matrons who never crossed the threshold leading from the nineteen-fifties to the sixties. A similar group of ladies had given *me* a Cola Hour back when I was just out of college and thrilled to be getting married. At the time, the most important thing had been to get at least eight place settings of every pattern chosen down at the local department store.

"I want my fine china more than anything," the girl had recently told me, her forehead glazed in acne. "Our pattern is Eternal by Lenox." She said the words in a dreamy way, a hypnotic way that suggested she wouldn't wake up until that first time she found her Eternal on the top shelf coated in dust. The happy ending comes if she can look at the dishes and laugh, and wonder why young couples don't ask for something like a washer and dryer, a car battery that never dies. If the dishes strike some distant unfulfilled yearning, then the future may not be so bright. I told her I also had picked a pattern by Lenox: Solitaire. She had squealed and clapped her hands. She knew my pattern. It had been one of her early considerations.

I call Sarah, who is responsible for this date in the first place, but there's just the cute little message on her machine, Sarah and hubby singing "Hey Ho Nobody Home." I hang up and dial the blind date's number, my mind void of pictures as the ring sounds in some unknown house/apartment/condo while some unknown man is stepping from the shower or pulling up his socks (cotton? nylon? black? white?) or driving to pick up his blind date. His machine answers but says nothing at all, just beeps.

"You be the giant," Jeffrey says, a rolled-up newspaper in his hand. "I'm gonna knock you out and steal the golden chicken."

"Fe, fi, fo, fum," I say for the hundredth time today and go stand on the hope chest (the giant's castle) at the foot of my bed. It's only been two years since I pulled that last brand-new set of wedding sheets from the chest. Now I use it as a storage place for cast-offs: baby blankets and squeaker toys, the hunting knife and heavy flannel shirt Nick forgot to pack. I'm thinking I'd like to climb in the chest and ignore the fact that any minute a complete stranger will be at my door.

Now Jeffrey is pretending to climb, head tilted back as he stares up at me. He's swinging a small tree limb he somehow smuggled into the house. "On guard!" He points to a stain on the carpet and says it's a crocodile. We've changed scripts just that fast. I'm Captain Hook and he's Peter Pan. I always get the sinister roles: witches and ogres and evil stepmothers. I give Snow White the poisoned apple and I make Sleeping Beauty touch the spindle and I talk Pinocchio out of going to school. I indulge my child's fantasy life despite the recent comments I've received about how this might not be healthy. My aunt Lenora has suggested that this is how he's (she leans close to whisper) *dealing with divorce*, these *violent* games.

Lenora is someone who got more education (one course here, another course there) than she could find room for in her head and has spent her whole adult life deleting whatever doesn't match her own opinion. "Give me a weekend and I could straighten him out," Lenora once told my mother, to which my mother simply replied, *Oh dear*. Lenora's own son has chosen a sort of evangelical route (having driven away a perfectly normal wife) and now spends his weekends in front of the Family Dollar store, handing out the religious poetry that he spent the rest of the week composing. I have always wanted to tell Lenora to go to hell. I can tell that, more than anything, my dear peace-loving mother wants to say, "Lenora, go to hell." But out of kinship or some distant childhood love, she just says things like, "Oh really, Lenora, he's just a little boy."

Still, in spite of my mother's loyalty, Lenora has planted the seed, and doubts are beginning to flourish. Just the other day my mother turned, her eyes narrowed in Lenora fashion, and said, "Doesn't it bother you that you always get the *negative* parts? You know, do you ever wonder if Jeffrey blames you, if he sees you as the *antagonist*?" That was Lenora's word for sure. Lenora had once made it perfectly clear that though Nick had left me, she thought I was the one to blame. *A man who is not well cared for will up and leave.*

I am being devoured by the crocodile when the doorbell rings. Jeffrey gets there first, his Ninja Turtle headgear in place. Phil is tall and fresh-looking, crisp as a stalk of celery. He extends his hand in a firm and cool shake and steps inside, navy wool socks and loafers, khakis and an oxford cloth shirt, narrow knit tie, circular brown frame glasses; he's the kind of man I always wanted to date in college, the kind of man Nick would size up quickly as a snob, a prep, a wimp. His eyes fix on me only a second and then he is looking around the room at the trophies and pictures and videotapes strewn about on the floor. I turn and catch a glimpse of myself in the hall mirror and quickly reach to pull the hot rollers from my hair.

"Sorry," I say and he looks at the rollers, nods and smiles; he thinks I'm apologizing for my hair. "But I don't have a sitter. She had an accident at school. There was just no way to get anyone else."

"Oh." He looks at Jeffrey, then looks back at me and shrugs. "So, we'll all go." He is wearing some kind of cologne which I don't recognize; Nick always said cologne was for somebody with something to hide. I'm not sure what else he is hiding but any disappointment is covered well.

"Yeah! Let's go. Let's go." Jeffrey runs and pulls his jacket from the low hook by the stairs.

"Are you sure?" I ask and he nods again. He is freshly shaven and not a scratch on his face. He looks like someone (a good guy or prince) out of one of Jeffrey's books; I keep expecting him to turn to the side and become the flat straight edge of a picture page or maybe just blow away and join the ankle-deep leaves as we walk through the yard. "Fe, fi, fo, fum," Jeffrey is saying as he crawls into the back seat. Phil holds open my door and I get in. When I look at my house, porch light and living room light on, I have an odd sense of guilt, like I'm breaking a rule or a law. It feels like *I'm* the one running away from home, only it's not so easy with a thirty-four-pound walking, talking superhero.

I imagine Phil had planned to take me somewhere else, maybe the tiny dark Greek restaurant on the other side of town, a place for couples and whispers. I imagine that with Jeffrey in the back, bumping against the seat in beat with his rendition of "Fe, fi, fo, fum," that Phil has thought better of disrupting that quiet dark meeting place for lovers and has made a quick turn into Captain Buck's Family Seahouse. And so here we are, nets on the ceiling and all furniture vinylized. I stir my iced tea round and round, the red plastic tumbler wet against my hand.

"Rather violent, isn't it?" Phil asks, and I jerk to attention, certain that he has seen my thoughts, my recounting of the final legal session that granted me divorce and child custody. For a single dollar (truly a rare bargain) I could have bought back my maiden name but declined since Jeffrey was stuck with the married one. Phil is talking about Hansel and Gretel and the way Jeffrey has delivered it, the mean ugly witch pushed into the oven and gassed, charred to a crisp. I don't tell how many times in the past week I've sat in the pantry, cackling and then screaming at the victorious Hansel.

"It's the same old story," I say and nod when Jeffrey asks to go and look at the aquarium on the far wall, a huge tank with glowing tropical fish. I watch him dash through the restaurant, barely missing a waitress with a tray piled high with fried food, oysters, shrimp, or clams, they all look the same with the thick golden batter, *calabash style* it is called. "I mean, when I was a kid, the witch landed in the oven."

"Yeah," Phil says and glances around, his fingers clasped loosely on the grease-shined oilcloth. "I guess you're right, but they are horrible stories, aren't they?"

"I don't know." I take a sip of tea and stare at the menu. Other than today's special broil, everything is fried; the question is how much fried can you take—small, medium, large, or deluxe? I can't imagine that Phil will order anything fried; I can't imagine that he's ever even been here before. "There are bad things that happen all over; why should fairy tales be excluded?" Phil is studying me and with his cool glance, I hear Sarah, the final advice/reprimand/instructions for this date: *Don't get all serious or maudlin, you know? The guy has never had kids so don't talk about Jeffrey the whole time and for God's sake don't talk about how the world is going to hell.* Easy for her to say since her little *hey ho* world is not.

"What I mean is—" I force a laugh. "Well, it's just easy for things to go too far in either direction." And I begin telling him about taking Jeffrey to see a little production of "Jack and the Beanstalk," where the story was not even recognizable. The giant, instead of falling to his death, climbs from the beanstalk and upon reaching the bottom is struck with amnesia and becomes a big-time land developer while poor Jack the hero fights the infiltration of shopping malls. I had taken Jeffrey straight home and read him the *real* version. Then we spent the rest of the evening with me falling to my earth-shattering death from the cedar chest.

Phil nods and it looks as if he might want to compliment this new version of "Jack and the Beanstalk" when up walks our waitress with Jeffrey right behind her. "I thought he must belong to you," she says when Jeffrey crawls up beside me. "He's having a time with those fish." The waitress is probably right out of college, probably spending a carefree summer before graduate school or career planning. Her face is smooth as silk, her gestures animated as she stands there in her black stretch pants and nautical top. "Now what can I get you?" she asks, and I watch Phil take her in, from the wild dark tresses to the tiny white sneakers. He smiles at her and orders the broiled flounder. I ask if I can get boiled shrimp *just like it would be in the shrimp cocktail only bigger*, and she has to go to the kitchen and ask. Jeffrey realizes for the first time that the fish that swim around in aquariums or talk, like in *The Little Mermaid*, could just as easily be the fish that get eaten, so we finally settle on a hamburger.

"Haven't read any cow stories, I guess," Phil says and he and the waitress grin at each other. They have met before, it seems; it was at a big New Year's party hosted by a friend of his who is a relative of hers.

"You were about to go to France, I believe," he says, and she turns, her side to me as she talks to Phil.

"I went," she says. "It was great. Better than what I'm doing now, which is applying to law schools. How about you, still pushing computers?" Phil laughs and leans back in his chair. He is relaxed and amused.

"Small world, isn't it a small world?" they both keep say-ing and looking to me for confirmation. Yes, I say. Yes it is a small world.

"So," Phil and I both say when our waitress leaves us in a wake of silence. We go back to the one topic of conver-sation that is safe and certain, Sarah and Dave, the friends who arranged this date. I barely know Dave and he barely knows Sarah, but it is enough to get by. I tell him that I've known Sarah ever since I moved here, that our class-rooms at the junior high are next door to each other. I met her in the parking lot the day I went for my interview. He keeps waiting, face animated as he anticipates some cute anecdote of it all: Sarah and I collide and our purses spill and our papers blow away or maybe I slip on a banana peel and land on the hood of her car. But nothing. It was a simple meeting where I said that I had grown up just thirty miles away and now my husband had been transferred here to oversee the construction of a new subdivision. Phil, it turns out, set up the computer system for Dave's podiatry clinic.

"I asked him," Phil says, our waitress within earshot, "why you'd ever choose feet for a living." Both of them burst out laughing, and I laugh out of beat, a little too late.

"So," Phil says when Betsy (the waitress) disappears be-hind the big bubbling aquarium. "I kind of like that new 'Jack and the Beanstalk.' "

"But what's next?" I ask. I look at him and keep thinking the words *perfect* and *manicured*. He is as clean and neat as a putting green, his fingernails rounded and filed to outline the balls of the fingers. I catch myself enjoying the clean brisk smell of his cologne, admiring the smoothness of his face. "How about," I say and take a sip of my tea, "if the evil witch in 'Hansel and Gretel' joins a support group?"

He laughs. "Then there's a spinoff group for daughters and sons of witches."

"The queen in 'Snow White' becomes a nice grandmotherly type?"

"It could happen," he says. I can't tell if his jolly mood is simply a part of him or spurred by his contact with Betsy. He's taking his time with his food, planning to stay awhile, it seems. Our booth looks out over the parking lot and the bypass. Jeffrey's face is pressed against the glass as he looks through the reflection of the room (a group of loud-talking middle-aged women behind us) and into the night. Heat spreads from his plump fingers, fogging the window.

An unbearable silence falls again (we've run out of cute ways to rehabilitate the evil characters), and it's difficult *not* to listen to the four women sitting across from us, their heads ringed in cigarette smoke as they pick through their mounds of batter and fries. They have already agreed at great length that anyone who burns the flag should receive the death penalty; they cannot imagine such a desecration happening, being *allowed* to happen in this country. "Let them just move in with the Communists," one of them is saying. "Just get out of our country if you disagree." I feel my chest tightening, my need to scream rising. Rewrite the fairy tales *and* the Constitution, I want to yell, go for the Gettysburg Address. Rewrite the Bible. I feel my grip tightening on my fork and I have that urge to drive it into the table, each tine sinking through the oilcloth with a pop. The Klan marches sixty miles from here. A five-year-old gets raped in a department store. There's about to be a war. Marriages fall apart like worn-out seams, and children's hearts get ripped along the edges where the threads won't give, and all you can talk about is a piece of cloth, a star-spangled *symbol*. If you burn your marriage certificate are you still married? If you burn your birth certificate are you still alive? If you lose your divorce papers is the decree null and void? Are you sentenced to return to that failed life?

I realize I've diced my food to bits but Phil doesn't notice; he smiles at Betsy as she fills the glasses of the women close by and then watches as she moves back towards the kitchen. Now the women are discussing with great fury the *hideous atrocity* which I soon figure out is Roseanne Barr and her rendition of the "National Anthem."

"Baseball, baseball," Jeffrey says and clicks his spoon against his milk glass, his voice an echo to one of the women who has told *where* it all took place. Phil raises his hand to Betsy and points to his empty water glass. She grins and steps out from the waitress station—a dark hall with a pay phone and a driftwood sculpture. Her stomach shows smooth and white as she reaches for the water pitcher. Phil is noticing, too. I hand Jeffrey a tissue and shake my head firmly, but he just laughs and goes back to what he was doing.

"Nose stuff," Jeffrey says when I shake my head again and pull his hand away. Betsy wrinkles her nose in disgust and then gives me a sympathetic smile, fills Phil's glass. "Ooh yuk," Jeffrey adds, and I encourage him to finish his meal or sit quietly, to count the cars that pass on the by-pass, to see if he can name all seven dwarfs, all seven Von Trapp children, the past fifteen presidents, all the states and their capitals.

"She grabbed herself you know where," one of the women nearby says, while Phil and the waitress share a laugh. I feel the room closing in, the air getting thick. Phil is still look-ing at Betsy. He looks like he's in a trance, like the Prince when Cinderella enters the ballroom, the Prince when he finds Snow White in her glass coffin, the *Prince* when he makes his way to Sleeping Beauty's bedside.

"Crotch," I say and swing around to face the table of women. The volume of my voice surprises me and Phil sits back, knife raised. "She grabbed her crotch." I shake my fork with each word. "It is a common gesture in baseball. Men have been doing it for years."

"Well, it was disgusting," the woman continues and turns from me as if I weren't present. Her friends all nod, cheeks bulging with calabash goulash. "A man has to do that." She receives another round of nods and turns back to me.

I feel Jeffrey slipping down to the floor of the booth and crawling past my legs. I feel helpless to stop him. "A man has to adjust hisself and it's not nice for the world to take notice."

"That's right," another swallows and says. "He can't go excusing himself each time he needs to adjust." Jeffrey has gone back to his spot by the aquarium now. His mouth is moving in mimicry of the fish. "Men have different needs. They always have."

"Well, what if I *need* to adjust myself?" I ask. "What if I have to keep adjusting my breasts all the time? Let's just say that I can't keep them properly housed inside my bra. What if my butt cheeks just will not stay in place?"

"Well, I *never*."

"I think we'll have the check," Phil says. The tips of his shiny ears are crimson. I watch Jeffrey, whose face is pressed against the aquarium glass on the opposite side. From here he looks immersed and misshapen, his face long and wavy. "Yo, fish," he says and licks the glass. Phil is watching me, his eyes pleading that I just let it all drop, while the table of women wait for me to make my move. Betsy has dashed off swiftly to Phil's rescue, her fingers rapidly figuring the bill for a hamburger barely touched and a plate full of mutilated shrimp I have rolled over and over in a cocktail sauce bath. My heart races as I watch Jeffrey twirling in the drapes. Betsy has signed the tab, "Have a wonderful evening. Come again soon!" in large rambling script, the loops of her letters as open as her young face. Phil smiles and hands her two twenties. He'll be back all right. There is electricity enough to light the building. She will give him excitement. He will give her stability. They will give each other warmth in a dark room.

I excuse myself to go untwist Jeffrey from the drapes. The women turn and watch, still expecting something from me. I want to swing around and grab my crotch but I keep walking, my hands reaching for my baby, his face and hands sticky with catsup. He says that the witch was behind the drapes and now he has got her locked in the oven and it's just a matter of time. The witch must burn. I pull him over to the door of the restaurant and wait for Phil, who is writing on what looks like a business card. He carefully tucks the card in his coat pocket and, after nodding to the table of women, joins me. I avoid looking at him for the time being. I know that I will apologize, that I will say *thank you for the meal*, that I will offer to pay for Jeffrey's, but for the moment I feel paralyzed. There is a sign in Uncle Buck's window advertising a Thanksgiving special and I toy with the thought of calabash-style turkey.

As soon as I step outside I feel sick, a cool sweat breaking out on my face and neck. I'd rather stretch out full length on the sidewalk and slip into a coma than to get in this man's car and try to carry on a conversation. Against my better judgment, I ease down and sit on the curb, head between my knees. Jeffrey spins around, a fake sword drawn and splitting the air. "I am Arthur! I am Arthur," he says. "I pulled this sword from that stone!"

"Are you okay?" Phil asks and after a few awkward moments, his feet shuffling beside me, he sits. He reaches inside his coat as if checking his pocket and then, reassured, he clasps his cool hands on his knees. "Dave told me you haven't had an easy year." I turn, startled. He is showing genuine concern. He has a pot on his back burner, a slow simmer of a phone number and so it's easier to be kind. I know that feeling; I remember it well. It seems I had more friends than I had ever had when I decided to get married just because I felt so confident that I had something. It wasn't threatening for me to be kind to someone. I didn't have to worry about what I'd do if that person took it the wrong way or wanted more from me. *I'm engaged*, or *I'm married*, that's all I had to say. For years, that's all I had to say, didn't even need to say it, it was obvious. And now that I'm single, legally free, everything seems threatening. I feel myself losing control, about to cry at this totally inconvenient moment.

"See if you can spin around like that again, Sir Arthur, see if you can count to twenty," Phil says, somehow knowing I need the extra time to get myself together.

"I'm sorry the night hasn't been more fun," he says.

"Well, it's not *your* fault." I force a laugh. "I'm certainly not the best company to keep."

"We all have our turns," he says and stands, offers me a

hand. "Some of us abuse old women in seafood joints." He pulls me up.

"And some of us pick up young waitresses."

"You noticed," he says. I nod, reach for Jeffrey's hand, and pull him along. Phil apologizes over and over on the ride home but I tell him there's no reason. I shake his cool hand and thank him for dinner. I imagine his picture ripped from a storybook—a two-dimensional prince—as he stands and waits for us to get inside. I turn the lock as Jeffrey bounds down the hall to his room. He names a dwarf each time he slaps his hand against the wall.

I'm sure Phil will drive back to the restaurant or to a phone booth, little card clutched in his hand. He will certainly call Betsy within the next twenty-four hours. She is just starting out, probably uses plastic milk crates to support her bed, a soft mattress draped with mismatched sheets and pillows. She doesn't trip over Ninja Turtles and Weebles in the middle of the night if she can't sleep and has to get up and walk around for a while. She doesn't feel herself needing to stick her head in the freezer and count to fifty. She's still waiting to begin, waiting to choose her patterns. There's no slate to wipe clean, no fears about having done (or doing) *irreparable damage to a young psyche*, and not just *a* young psyche, but *the* young psyche, *the* person you love more than anyone else on earth, the person who turns your mistake into something you wouldn't change.

*   *   *

It is very late when I hear Jeffrey get up. The night light glows behind him, and he looks so small as he scampers down the dark hallway to my room. Twice I have awakened to find him standing there staring at me, his hands on the edge of the mattress.

"Mom?" He is beside my bed now, his hand full of leftover candy from Halloween. "Who was that man?"

"Just a friend of Sarah's," I say, and he is totally satisfied with that answer. His trust in me is complete. If it weren't, he'd never give me the *bad* parts to act out. And what's wrong with acting out the bad parts? What's wrong with Jack getting rid of the giant? And why shouldn't Hansel and Gretel kill the witch in self-defense? Hooray for Dorothy, the wicked witch is dead. Then you just turn the page and start all over.

"You want to hear a story?" he whispers.

"Sure," I say. He crawls up, his breath like candy corn.

"It's a scary one."

"Scarier than 'Hansel and Gretel'?" I ask and he nods, moves in closer.

"This is about 'The Three Billy Goats Gruff,'" he says and begins, his voice a rapid whisper, his heart beating quickly each time he says *trip trap trip trap trip trap* and describes the old troll who threatens to eat the goats.

"Are you scared?" he asks, his sticky hand groping to find my face.

"A little," I say. "Are you?"

"Oh, no." He wiggles in closer. "I'm the biggest billy goat of all." His breath quickens as he repeats the verse, hand clutching my arm. I close my eyes and hug him tighter. *Who goes there? Trip trap trip trap trip trap*. I imagine a postcard scene, cartoon-green grass and a brilliant blue sky. Now all we have to do is cross the bridge.

Carnival Lights

I never slept with Donnie Wilkins like everybody says I did. I could go and straighten it all out, I guess. I could sit down with the phone book and pick through the names of everybody I know, call and give my speech, my explanation about how they've got the wrong idea about me. I would say, "Hey, this is Lori Lawrence, you know Mr. Lawrence who is co-owner of that new grocery store where everything's all natural? I'm his daughter. I just graduated from the high school. I carried a flag in the marching band. I've helped flip the sausage patties at the Kiwanis pancake supper since I was eleven." And then I'd pause because of course they'd know who I was. It isn't like this is some metropolis we live in. There are no more than eight thousand people here, and so once you figure in marriage and friends of friends, it gets real small.

People don't even expect the new grocery store to make it, that's how small it is. Then my dad will be out beating the pavements and I'll have to hear that old *this is why we are so proud you're going to college* speech. There were only seventy-five people in my graduating class, and if I hadn't been one of them (like I honestly feared for a while), my parents would've died fourteen hundred times.

Nobody needs to be told who I am. Everybody knows my mama is Sandy Lawrence. She used to be Sandy Leech and, yes, we have heard *all* of those parasite jokes. We made a bunch of them up ourselves. My mother is the little plump woman who always wears clogs and who will fill in and drive a schoolbus if somebody's sick. Otherwise she is a secretary at the courthouse, vital information at her finger-tips. We hear things over the dinner table that don't even get in the paper until the next day. Everybody knows she married my dad the same night she graduated from high school because she was afraid he'd be drafted. Everybody *also* knows that I was born exactly—give or take a day or two—nine months later. She says that though this course of action would *not* be good for a girl like me, it was the best thing she could have done in 1972 and she has never regretted her decision. She says I might think the world was so very different eighteen years ago but within these city limits, except for the fashions and music, it was pretty much the same. The Lions Club was selling light bulbs and brooms and the Civitans were selling fruitcakes. Her parents *made* her go to Methodist Youth Fellowship, which is why she had left me to my own free will. She grew up with old parents and once said that she had decided to break that mold and several others; she didn't want us to be afraid to ask her questions and she didn't want us to have to bury her before we got out of high school. Speaking of her old parents, Granddaddy Leech lives with us; you know him, old Herman Leech, who used to grow tobacco and now doesn't know what day it is or who he is.

I've got a little brother, Bill, who is a royal pain. His way of getting on Mama's nerves is to pick on Granddaddy and call him names even though Granddaddy doesn't know the difference. Daddy says this is Bill's way of dealing with the way Granddaddy has changed. At least that's what Daddy said over the holidays in between learning how to pronounce the various kinds of yuppie lettuce he was suddenly responsible for buying and selling.

"People want more than just iceberg," he said every hour or so. Mama said she didn't know why people were suddenly so hepped up on maroon-colored wilted lettuce and she didn't know how Granddaddy's falling off could possibly explain why Bill had draped the old man's head with a woman's nylon hose and Christmas tinsel. She also wanted to know where Bill got that nylon hose. He's just two years younger than I am but you'd never guess it. He looks like he ought to be in the seventh grade rather than just out of the tenth. I sure wouldn't go out with him if I were a girl other than his sister. We look a lot alike—thick curly hair and compact bodies, eyes too big and sad for the rest of us. It's the kind of look that goes better on a girl.

People say that for somebody so short, I've got a large chest and that I should've made cheering squad and would've if I hadn't had that fight with Bonita Inman when I was in the tenth grade and she called my daddy a fruit pusher (though hoping for a break in the business, he was still just manager at Food Lion at the time). You can imagine how everybody took it from there and got to saying fruit pimp, gigolo. They made awful jokes about bananas and cucumbers. It was nothing to take sitting down, and I got sent home with one-day suspension for fighting at the bus stop. A clump of Bonita's hair was still in my fist when my father choked up in that old Chevette. The worst part was that I couldn't tell him *why* I'd socked Bonita in the face and made her nose bleed down a blouse which she had broadcasted all day long was brand new from that new store in the mall where the mannequins are painted silver and don't have faces. "Tell me what happened, Lori," my mother said that night. "You can tell us the truth." My dad was standing there with her, and I made up some silly story about Bonita calling me a name so ugly I couldn't repeat it. You just don't look your father (or the woman who loves him) in the face and say he's been the butt of penis jokes for two days running.

*   *   *

I did *not* sleep with Donnie Wilkins even though I wanted to. He's a nice guy and I'm a nice girl. I mean, I've only had one boyfriend other than Donnie. I went with Mike Tyler my junior year for one month, the highlight of our relationship being the Sunday nights I exercised my free will and we stood out behind the Methodist church during youth fellowship and kissed. I told him that if he could keep his mouth shut, I'd go with him, otherwise forget it. Ours was a brief relationship which ended with him telling people that he had given me seven hickeys and had undone my shirt to get a feel three times. Of course that wasn't true, only further proof of his inability to keep his trap shut, but still there it was, the beginning of my reputation being sucked down the drain.

Donnie's dad is the school guidance counselor, a tall skinny man who looks like he's made out of Tinkertoys. It was in late November, around the time everybody was taking the SAT, when he told me that I had a lot of natural talent for putting things together and taking them apart. "If you were a boy," he said and looked over at Donnie's mama who assists him at his job, her little half glasses swinging from a chain around her neck, "I'd tell you to go to trade school, become a mechanic." I keep hoping that women's lib will be what follows the all-natural grocery in my hometown, but as of yet, people are still doing the HIS and HER types of things.

Everybody in school made jokes about the Wilkinses being the guidance counselors (her title is Assistant Guidance Counselor). People said that *really* there's just *one* of them and that he/she has many personalities like in that movie, *Sybil*. I tried not to think about all that while I looked at them, their button-down shirts the exact same shade of blue.

"I'd like to be an engineer," I offered. "Or an architect." When he talked of my *natural talent* it wasn't like he was telling me some big news I didn't already know. I knew the first time I ever sat down with a can of Lincoln Logs that I had this special *aptitude*, as they say. Lincoln Logs and Legos are why I stayed in the baby-sitting business as long as I did. I have a special aptitude all right. I could look at him and *know* how many cans of Tinkertoys it would take to duplicate his body. Mrs. Wilkins was harder to figure.

"But you're a girl." Mrs. Wilkins inched her chair closer to her husband's and peered down at my test scores. I know what she was really peering at was the front of my notebook where I'd written her son's name in big block letters. I loved Donnie Wilkins and had for a long time. Even when I was kissing Mike behind the church, I was loving Donnie Wilkins. He had finally started loving me just two months before, when we found ourselves sitting together at a football game. The band wasn't performing because the field was so muddy, but we wore our uniforms anyway. They finally called the game on account of rain, and we were about the only people left in the stands, our heads under his denim jacket and leaned in real close. It could have been a toothpaste or breath mint commercial on TV; it was that good.

"You are a girl with a grade point total that falls just a little above class average, and so I suggest you take the clerical courses out at the Technical Institute and see how you fare in a setting of higher learning before committing yourself," Mr. Wilkins said. His "just a little above class average" was a 93 so I knew he was not telling the whole truth. And everybody knew that I would have had an even higher average except I had received an 'F' for everything I missed on that day I was suspended two years before. I knew that what The Counselors were really thinking was that someone like me would need financial assistance to go to college and it was just too damn much trouble to fill out the forms.

"You think I should take a course like you took?" I asked Mrs. Wilkins and watched her bristle, her lips as thin as a paper cut. I turned and watched the principal on the other side of the glass partition. Mr. Sinclair was attractive in an odd way, sort of a prehistoric way. When he first moved here last year, the rumors raced that he'd once had a part on a detergent commercial that was filmed in New York, but he announced, in a joking sort of way, in the first assembly that this was not true. (He had only *tried out* for it.) He was married and had three small children.

He had been a wrestler in college and it showed. He had a real thick neck and walked with his legs apart. A lot of the girls like Mr. Sinclair's looks, but I much prefer Donnie Wilkins's type, thin and graceful, smart-looking. Mr. Sinclair is what some people might call a jock. If I had to give an opinion I'd say he's all right for his age, which my best friend, Jennifer Morgan, says must be forty or so. At the ball games his wife just sits there quiet as a mouse with children hanging all over her, while he stands and waves his broad hand at the people in the stand like *he* might've made that eighty-yard touchdown instead of Scooter Clark. My dad says that Mr. Sinclair is much too hard on the fruit in the grocery store and oftentimes eats as much as he buys while shopping. To his credit, though, or so my dad says, he's a man's man, an iceberg lettuce man. No flaccid leaves for him.

"I *was* in a clerical position," Mrs. Wilkins said, again with that strained look. "I've gone back to school for two summers now. It is hard work." She smiled a fake smile.

"She's enrolled in a class right now." Mr. Wilkins looked at her and grinned. "She has to go at night and that's hard work. She's a modern woman."

And you just got voted most desirable fat man on the planet, I was thinking and had to look away.

"That's right." Mrs. Wilkins nodded her head modestly, returned his smile and then continued. "You could start out at Tech and whether or not you pursue school after that . . . well, time will tell." She had one of those faces that is easily forgotten, a powdered white face that looks like a ray of sunshine has never shone her way, mousey, plain, all those words you put with little pointed-looking women, waist cinched in *just so*, cheeks sucked in *just so*. I sat there and imagined her to be somebody who washed her hands and couldn't stop.

While The Guidance Counselors sat there and talked about what I should do with my life, I sat there wondering how this pair had ever come to give birth to my Donnie. I was thinking that Mrs. Wilkins probably had tissue *folded* in tiny squares in some hidden compartment of her purse and she handwashed her underwear (she would say panties) but never touched the crotch when checking to see if they were dry. She was the kind of woman who complained about public toilets and hovered her butt over the john like a helicopter and sprayed without any thoughts about who would come in and want to use that commode next. I hate when women do that, too good just to wipe off the seat or even cover it over several times with toilet paper. I made myself laugh while picturing Mrs. Wilkins's mousey little *panties* pulled down around those snow white ankles while she crouched and sprayed the floor of the girls' bathroom, where the walls tell you to go and do things I've never done but have thought about, and the air is thick with cigarette smoke.

"Is that my Donnie's name you've got on your note-book?" Mrs. Wilkins asked. Her eyes matched her beige skirt, shoes, and hair. Mr. Wilkins shifted in his seat, and it hurt me to think of those knobby bones rolling beneath him.

"Peggy," Mr. Wilkins said. "Let's keep this discussion on Miss Lawrence's test performance."

"Very well," she said. "But you ought to know that Donnie will be going off to school next fall."

"I know that," I told her and pushed my chair back from the table. I could look through the glass partition and see everybody milling around in the hall, getting ready to dash through those big double doors with that three o'clock bell. I was supposed to meet Donnie out in front of the school so we could ride in Red Smith's new Jeep Cherokee. "I'm going off to school, too."

"You are?" Mrs. Wilkins asked and scanned my aptitude test again as if she'd overlooked some major fact. "Where are you going and what in?"

"In what, dear." Mr. Wilkins patted her hand and shook his head. Her cheeks flushed for a second but then she came back around to her natural pasty color and was right back in there with Mr. Tinkertoy. Just as the two of them were closing in on me, the bell sounded and I bolted. I started to tell Donnie how weird I thought his folks were, but by the time we were all alone I decided I'd rather kiss him instead. We were in the back seat of the Jeep, his blue-jean jacket around my shoulders. "So what do your parents think about us going together?" I asked right when Red Smith leaned out the door of the Time Out and motioned for us to come inside—it was our turn for the pinball machine. I could tell by the look on Donnie's face that I'd hit a rough spot. "We've been going together two months, one week, and two days, but they act like they've never heard of me."

"I don't know." He shrugged. "They know we're friends but my parents are kind of weird about those things." There was a pause and then he had all his reasons together and started talking real fast. "You know, they're afraid I'll change my mind about going off next year or something so I just don't tell them a whole lot. You can see that, can't you?" I nodded because he had the purest, clearest emerald green eyes I'd ever seen and nice full lips. He had a mature-looking razor stubble, too, particularly up against somebody like Red, who had skin like a baby's butt. I nodded and leaned in close enough to breathe in the scent of his Obsession, which all the boys in my class were wearing if they could scrape up the money to buy some. I was thinking that for excitement his parents probably sat in ramrod fashion and spanked each other's palms with rulers or something. They probably conjugated verbs over the dinner table. She probably had to get his permission to sit her modern mousey self down. He probably had to floss his teeth before she'd kiss him. I was thinking, *Your parents are queer as a three-dollar bill*, but what I said was, "Of course, Donnie. Why, that makes lots of sense. I really like how you smell."

For Christmas I gave Donnie Obsession body shampoo (which my mother thought was a little personal until I explained how it was no different from what she had once known as *soap on a rope*) and a key chain with his initials (my father's suggestion, something about how a man should always have something jingling in his pocket). That, like everything on the planet, reminded Bill of a dirty joke, and he got sent out of the room even though everybody (including Granddaddy) had laughed. Donnie gave me a pen and pencil set (gift choice of The Counselors, I'm sure). But secretly, what we gave each other was a solemn vow that very soon, as soon as we felt comfortable with the idea, we'd go somewhere where we could be all alone and take our clothes off. We didn't make any promises beyond that.

Over the holidays, Bill and I sat up one whole night watching the "Madonna Marathon" on MTV. I was studying the way she moved and took her clothes off. Bill sat there trying to act like he wasn't about to start drooling. Then we both got distracted by circling headlights in the parking lot across the street from our house. For years that lot had been the meeting spot for people fooling around, or so my parents always joked. They never named names but it was obvious they knew some things. "What do you think we did before we could afford a big television and cable?" my dad often asked, and she grinned at him. It was possible she was grinning about something *else* they did which I couldn't bear to think about. It gave me the creeps to imagine my parents in a hot naked embrace, especially now that I was planning my *own* unvirgining.

Bill and I had sat and waited for cars to come before, but this was the first time we'd actually witnessed a meeting. We didn't have any lights turned on other than the TV, so it was easy enough to kneel by the window and watch the two cars pull into spaces side by side. The dark station wagon's engine cut off, lights out, door opened. Bill was breathing too close to me, his breath like nacho Doritos, and he fogged the glass. By the time we stopped shoving each other, the other car had driven off and we had missed seeing who had moved from one car to another. Bill had the bright idea that we'd sneak out to watch the return, but an hour later we both got caught up in Madonna's "Like a Virgin" video, and while we were trying to figure out why those weird-looking guys were wearing and stroking these really gross-out fake boobs while Madonna writhed on the bed, both cars disappeared. "That was a quickie," Bill said knowingly as he stared out into the empty lot. "Poor guy just couldn't keep going."

"What do you know?" I asked, and he turned to face me

just as seriously as if I'd asked him to explain condensation. He turned his head to one side and sighed.

"I know more than you know," he finally said and flipped open his wallet to show me a condom packet.

"Yeah, right," I said and examined the packet. "This must have come with the wallet." It said it was a size *large*, but I didn't say anything about that. Everybody I heard talking about condoms (people like Mike Tyler and Rowland Jones) talked about how they *needed* a size large. Yeah, right; like how have people gone all these years without the jumbo size? What boy is going to walk in and say give me a size *small*? I closed the Doritos and put the bag on the table. Madonna was writhing again to "Express Yourself," and I decided not to challenge Bill on his *knowledge* or his size; it was not a good time for me to be swapping stories, not to mention the fact that if he *had* done something, I didn't want to think about it. My head was already getting filled up with enough thoughts without one of Bill dancing the dance.

Vacation ended and Donnie and I still hadn't taken anything off. The Counselors had given him a long speech over the holidays (probably after they saw his body shampoo) about how he was too young for something serious and shouldn't be dating just one person. Everybody at school *knew* we were going steady, but neither of us ever came right out and said it. The only person who knew all about our plan was Jennifer Morgan, and she was sworn to secrecy. I knew what was going on with her, too, and that's what being best friends is all about. You've got the dirt on each other and it holds you tight like glue. Jennifer took the pill and Rowland Jones had put his hand up her bra right there in Chemistry while they were supposed to be washing some beakers they'd burned up real bad. If that's not insurance, there's no such thing.

It was February when Bill started calling Granddaddy "Paw Paw," all the while rapping and dancing around like M. C. Hammer, which drove my mother up the wall. It was right after the doctor said that Granddaddy would never ever be the same. It didn't matter what Bill called him, Granddaddy grinned great big. Paw Paw, Monterey Jack, Homer Simpson, it didn't make a dab bit of difference, except anything other than Granddaddy Leech made Mama bite her lip and turn away. The worse Granddaddy got, the more my parents talked about me going to college, and before I knew it they had me filling out all kinds of applications and financial aid forms they had ordered themselves. Nothing like a good sharp contrast between life and death to make people start planning out their futures. I knew then more than ever that Bill (yes, Bill) and I were a big hunk of my parents' future. It shocked me to think that when my mother was my very age, she and my dad were talking about their *future* together. It was hard to believe that such planning went into me and Bill and all those grocery store jobs.

Meanwhile Donnie said that he was tired of waiting for us to be together. He said if something didn't happen soon he'd die. My mother had once told me that there were lots of stories boys would tell to get what they wanted: explosions, blindness, wild-seed sowing, but somehow Donnie's reasons sounded real. There had been many nights when we could have easily kept right on going (he sure wanted to), but I just didn't want my first memory to be of a back seat.

Then we heard the carnival was coming to town, and we decided *that* was our perfect time. Everybody got to stay out late those nights since it was a rare event to have so much entertainment in town. The carnival came on a Wednesday afternoon, and by Thursday morning, they were already all set up in the big vacant lot across from the shopping center. It was what my daddy called a *snap-to* carnival. He said he'd stood right there in the grocery window and watched it all appear out of nowhere. On Friday night the carnival was going to kick off with The Retching Wretches, a local band whose lead singer was a girl who had once been our babysitter. Donnie and I had planned to meet all of our friends at the band's performance and then slip off and go for a drive; he said he had the perfect place for us to go. I knew it was the Royal Villa Inn out on Highway 301 (he had talked to Rowland Jones, who told Jennifer since they had been there before themselves), but I didn't let on that I knew. I had a black lace bra and underwear hidden in an empty box of Cheerios in my school locker.

"Those rides can't be safe," Mama said and wheeled Monterey Jack up to the table. This was on Friday morning, right after she'd informed us that we couldn't go to the carnival that night. "It's Granddaddy's birthday," she said and bent to kiss Granddaddy's cheek. "We decided late last night to do something special, have a few of the old neighbors in."

"But the band is playing." Bill said.

"You can go tomorrow night," she said.

"*Old* neighbors is right," Daddy patted Granddaddy's shoulder. He was ignoring our pleas. "Right, Pops?" Granddaddy just grinned great big and then focused on Bill, studied him as if he'd never seen him before. I could tell it made Bill uneasy. He had always been Granddaddy's favorite, and now the old man was looking at him like he had no earthly idea who he was. It was like our grandfather had already died and we were left with this big doll baby to remind us that he'd once been a part of our lives. It was getting hard for me to look at him, and the thought of a whole roomful of old people gave me the creeps.

Bill finally got tired of arguing about going to the carnival and balanced a spoon on Granddaddy's head. I probably would have laughed, but I was upset about having to tell Donnie I couldn't make our date. What if he thought I didn't *want* to take my clothes off with him? What if he thought I was having second thoughts? What if he couldn't get his parents' car a second night, how would we get to the Royal Villa Inn? Where was I going to hide my fancy underwear at home so that I'd have it for *Saturday* night?

I wrote Donnie a quick note while Bill and Jennifer and I waited for the school bus. I made it real mushy so he would believe what was the truth. Then I said that my grandfather, who was old and would probably die before too long (Bill had suggested I say Granddaddy was circling the drain), was having a birthday party and I had to be there. As wracked with grief as I was (Jennifer's suggestion), I couldn't keep our date. I said that I longed for our moment together, the one we had planned, the one that filled my every dream waking and sleeping. I said, "But it'll be worth the wait! It'll be Grrrrreat, you big bad Tiger" (also Jennifer's suggestion—she was very good at that kind of letter). He took it all real well, responding with a note wedged up in the vent slots of my locker that simply said "Tomorrow is the Day!" It was Jennifer's mission (if she could keep some sense about her while on a date with Rowland Jones) to keep an eye on Donnie just in case somebody decided to move in on my turf.

Granddaddy and his guests didn't know it was his birthday, but we celebrated all the same. Daddy brought home a bag of cherry tomatoes and made them look like little roses; he hollowed out a red cabbage and filled it with dip. It was all beautiful and everybody told him so, but all Granddaddy and his friends ate were the little pastel butter mints and the Cheetos that left their hands and mouths bright orange. Mama said that such a birthday celebration is like a funeral, a ritual for the living, so you'll feel like you've done the best you could. Bill sang *Happy Birthday, dear Paw Paw* and when Mama gave him a dirty look changed his song to *Happy Birthday, dear Burrhead*. Granddaddy grinned great big and then cried, his mouth twisting silently. By nine Granddaddy was tucked in bed and fast asleep.

While my parents shuttled all the guests back where they'd come from, I cleaned the kitchen. Bill actually offered to help me, balancing his niceness by calling me *asshole*. More and more, Bill was trying to get on my good side. He never would've admitted it, but he was terrified of girls. He knew that if he didn't hurry up and grow taller or get some facial or underarm hair, that he was in for a bumpy ride. He had a crush on Tanya Taylor, who was my fellow flag girl, and more than ever, he needed me.

Several times since the "Madonna Marathon," Bill and I had seen those same two cars pull up and park, the station wagon left behind while the other drove off down that dark road that led to Hermit's Crossing. Bill told me a lot of high school people went there, too. He waited for me to say something, and the way he looked at me it was almost like he knew about my plans. Bill said some older boys told him that you could find *things* out there: underwear and stockings and *things* you wouldn't want to touch. I had only seen Hermit's Crossing in the daylight. All it was was a little wooden bridge crossing a stream, but there were lots of stories about how it was haunted.

It was after ten when my parents got home and we all went to bed. I knew that Bill was probably already up and sneaking back in to watch MTV or to call one of those 900 numbers that had mysteriously appeared on our phone bill the month before. "What is this?" my mother had asked and handed the number to my dad. I don't know if she was accusing him or not. She had already called the number to see who answered and had gotten quite a shock. Then they called back for *him* to hear. "Good grief," he said. "You thought I'd called that?" They never even asked Bill about it, just assumed aloud that some *sordid* person had charged his *filth* to our number. Still, I did notice that every night before going to bed my mother adjusted the phone on the table just so; it seemed to me that it was positioned on the phone book in such a way that she'd know if it had been touched. "What kind of young girl takes such a job?" my mother had whispered to my father when she thought I wasn't paying attention. "And I wonder," she continued, "is she reading what she says or making it up right off the top of her head?" I didn't hear what he said to her but it was one of those times I wished I hadn't seen. She just sort of smiled and turned red. She pushed his arm and said, "Oh really, Jack," and then they kissed that slow close way that made me feel like I didn't belong on this earth. It seemed to me that every time she touched the phone book it was a signal for him to give her that look.

I lay there that night half waiting to hear Bill dialing. I was trying to picture myself in the act with Donnie, but I kept picturing my parents or the weird guys from the Madonna video instead. It was like I was watching a scrambled channel and I couldn't keep it focused on just me and Donnie. I must have been lying there for about a half hour when I heard a car pass and then the engine cut. I tiptoed out into the living room, expecting to see Bill perched in front of the window, binoculars up to his eyes, but he had fallen asleep. The figures on MTV were moving around in silence. The phone was exactly the same on the table. I knelt just as the other car drove off. I started to wake him but then I changed my mind. I needed some time to myself to think through things. I'm not one to ever go creeping around at night, so I'm not quite sure what came over me. It was like I had a sudden urge to sneak out. The next thing I knew I had my jacket on and was tiptoeing through the kitchen.

Quietly, I stepped out the back door and crept through

the side yard, following the edge of the parking lot so that I was always near some high shrubs. I sat watching the lot for what seemed like an hour. It was quiet out there, too chilly for any frogs or crickets to be calling. The station wagon was a Camry, black or dark blue or burgundy. (My dad said we were about the only people in town without a car that was made in Japan.) I tiptoed around, pressing my face against the windows, but I couldn't see anything. I was about to squat down and try to read the license number, when I saw headlights coming down Hermit's Crossing Road. My whole life I'd heard those stories about Hermit's Crossing and how that's where witches had been killed hundreds of years before. They said if you went and stood in front of the huge live oaks you'd hear the creaking of the ropes as they hung, hear the crackling of the fire as they burned. With a rush of gooseflesh I crouched down in the bushes and held my breath. I waited, barely breathing, while the other car pulled up beside the wagon. I couldn't see the driver at all. It was a Honda, but the color was difficult to figure in that light: white, yellow, pale blue. I felt my chest tighten like I might have to scream or laugh or something. I was about to run when the door on the passenger side opened and then I saw him, Mr. Sinclair, just as big and thick-necked as ever. "See ya, babe," he said. Then he clucked his tongue and said, "Mmmmm, mmmmm, mmmmm."

I felt all the blood pumping to my head, and every muscle

in my body tensed. He stood there in the dark empty parking lot and watched the Honda pull away, his keys jingling in his hand. The car rolled right by me, the tires kicking up sand. There was a piece of twine hanging out of the trunk like maybe it had been tied down or something, and then I realized that I had studied the twine, its ends painted fluorescent yellow, and had missed my chance to read the license. All I caught was a "booster club" bumper sticker, which everybody in town had bought to support the high school athletic department. It seemed like hours before Mr. Sinclair got in his own car and cranked the engine, the roar vibrating across the empty lot. I sat back and took a deep breath, the fumes from the Camry still in the air. My knees were shaking like they never had before, like rubber, like jelly. I didn't feel normal until I got inside and collapsed on Bill's pallet on the living room floor. "Bill." I shook him and he rolled towards me, let out a deep sigh. I shook him again but he shrugged me away. It took a good ten minutes before he was really awake, and in that time, I decided that I had some leverage and ought to use it. I told Bill everything I'd seen except *who* it was. He was begging. He was ready to do my household chores for a week, ready to pay me ten dollars.

"What kind of car was it?" he asked.

"A station wagon."

"The other car." He was getting impatient.

"A Honda."

"Oh, great." He sat up and pulled a bag of Doritos out from under the sofa. "Everybody drives a Honda. Was it an Accord or a Civic?"

"What do I look like, a car dealer?" I asked. I was enjoying myself. After all the times he had taped mine and Jennifer's conversations or tried to spy on me and Donnie, I had him where I wanted him.

"I'll just go out there myself," he finally said, tired of begging. "I'll go tomorrow night and every night until they come back." He wanted me to tell the end again, the part about *mmmmm mmmmm mmmmm*.

"Who said that?" he asked quickly, thinking he could trick me into saying, and we both fell out laughing. I had never felt so close to Bill, and I almost reconsidered and told him that it was Mr. Sinclair. There was even a part of me that wanted to tell him about mine and Donnie's plan, how we were in love and ready to make a move, *show* how we loved each other, but I let the moment pass. Bill seemed so vulnerable at night stripped down to a T-shirt and gym shorts, spots of Clearasil on his chin and forehead, but come morning he would be right back to his tricks. As much as we *wanted* to trust each other, we just couldn't. I closed my eyes and tried to conjure Donnie, but all I could see was Mr. Sinclair's thick neck and back moving up and down in a back seat, some unknown *babe* beneath him.

Donnie picked me up in his dad's new Chrysler at six the next night. My face was so flushed with nervousness that Mama kept asking if I was sick and pressing her hand up against my forehead. Bill had already left to go to the carnival with some boys his age, but I knew that he was planning to set up camp in the parking lot later that night. All day long he had talked about it, and all day long I was torn between the sick feeling I had thinking about Mr. Sinclair saying "Mmmmm mmmmm mmmmm" and the nervousness I felt when I put on that lace bra and underwear. I was terrified that my mother would see the lacy outline under my sweater.

"Have fun, kids!" Mama called as Donnie and I got in the car. My dad had gone to rent a movie, which is what they always did (or said they did) when Bill and I were both out. They rented movies we'd never heard of with stars who had either died or gotten real old and fat. I breathed a sigh of relief as I leaned into the plush leather seat. I had made it over the first hurdle. Donnie was all shaved and smelling of Obsession. I watched the key chain I'd given him dangle from the ignition as we drove to Shoney's. We were both nervous. Donnie asked for a booth by the window so we could look out at the carnival, where all the lights were coming on, the Ferris wheel moving in a circle as jumpy as our conversation. Donnie got the fried chicken plate and I got the salad bar. We started to have dessert but then passed as we watched the Bullet in the distance, the passenger cars on either end spinning and twisting. Everybody had talked about the Bullet at school. Dares had been made about who could ride it the most times without get-

ting sick. Scooter Clark had talked about how, the year before, he and Andy Hamilton had found all kinds of money
that had flown from pockets to the ground around the ride.

We walked from Shoney's, since it was hard to find a
parking spot. Donnie grabbed my hand, and his felt almost
as cold and clammy as my own. I kept waiting for him to
mention our plans, but instead he kept talking about how
pretty the moon was coming up in the distance and was I up
for riding the Bullet and did I really believe that there was
any such thing as a miniature horse only fourteen inches
high. "No, I don't believe it," I said just as we were passing
the trailer that said there *was* a fourteen-inch horse.

"What about The Headless Woman?" he asked. We
stopped and stood in front of the trailer, the voice on the
loudspeaker inviting us to come in and see this medical
miracle. The sloppy letters on the side of the trailer said she
had been decapitated in a car accident but was still living.
Donnie was waiting for me to say whether or not I wanted
to go. I shook my head no and we continued, past the Led
Zeppelin Laser Light Show (Jennifer had said that it was
the best part of the carnival), past the Sky Diver, past the
Haunted House where Andy Hamilton was working as a
werewolf. He perched up on the roof and jumped down on
each cart as it came out, couples screaming bloody murder
at the sight of his hairy mask. We stood there and watched
him work for a while. It was so funny we started to loosen
up with each other. I was feeling good, warm and happy

and almost ready to go somewhere and take my clothes off, when Donnie said that he had forgotten something important. I didn't have to be a rocket scientist to know what that *something* was, and the thought of our rendez-vous leading to *that* gave me a little shock. All night I had wanted to tell him about Mr. Sinclair but was waiting until the ride home when we'd already done what we were going to do. I didn't want him to think I was making suggestions.

I was relieved to find that the *something* I was think-ing (why would he keep them at home anyway?) was not what he meant. His something was that he was supposed to go over and speak to his parents, who had volunteered to oversee the high school booths. "Let's go on and get it over with," he said and pulled me away just as Andy jumped down on top of a middle-aged couple. The man pulled back his fist and was about to sock Andy, but the ticket taker stepped in to explain it was part of the ride.

The high school booths were at the far edge of the park-ing lot under a big tent that had been donated by Price Funeral Home. We passed by the shop projects and I saw Bill's TV table he had worked on so long. He had said it was a present for Granddaddy, and it made me sad to see it sitting there holding lamps made from Gallo wine jugs. I had wanted to take shop but everybody talked me out of it; I took Latin like a *bona puella* instead, though to hear The Counselors talk I had no business saddling myself with such collegiate courses. And speaking of Ms. *Femina Con-*

silium, there she was in all of her mousey glory. I saw her take me in from head to toe, and I wished she *could* see my lacy black bra through my sweater, complete with its little foam push-ups. I would have liked to shock her out of ramrod position. Instead I smiled politely and said nothing while Donnie bought some toll house cookies in a Baggie.

"Where's Dad?" Donnie asked.

"Oh, poor man," she said. "He just wasn't feeling well, said that all these lights and things spinning had made him feel sick, so I told him to go on home and rest."

"Oh." Donnie hesitated as if she had him under some kind of spell. "Well, how will you get home?"

"I've got the car," she said. "Your dad got a ride home. Oh, go on now, shoo." She waved her hand, smiling at Donnie and never once looking at me. "Have fun," she said. "Don't stay out too late. I have to close the booth but Dad will be home all night."

"Do you want to swap cars?" Donnie asked, forehead wrinkled.

"No, I'm fine." She was holding the cash box up to her chest like I might be aching to steal it. "Oh, but, Donnie," she called, "if you will, do bring me my seat cushion from the trunk. It's going to be a long night." She handed him the key, and that's when I saw her look at my breasts. "I'm right beside that Dumpster behind the drugstore."

"Be right back," he called and then pulled me towards the

parking lot. "As soon as we take her the cushion, we can go. I'm sorry I've been so quiet, but you know, I knew we had to come over here and I just wanted everything else out of the way." I felt his arm circle around my waist, his hand finding its way up the side of my sweater. "I can't wait," he whispered as we walked in and out of rows of cars. I was about to ask him where we were going when he grabbed me and kissed me like he never had before, my back thrown up against that filthy old Dumpster. I was out of breath and my heart was pounding when he stopped and opened the trunk. He was telling me how as long as he could remember his dad always got sick at things like this and left his mom to fend for herself. He said his mother had sat on a cushion ever since she had an accident and hurt her back. I heard myself asking what kind of accident, but I wasn't really thinking about his answer. I was thinking about that piece of twine dangling from the trunk, its ends flecked with yellow. I knew before looking down at the bumper the exact placement of the booster club sticker. I thought of her then, thin white body beneath Mr. Sinclair, her hands on his broad muscular back, her heart beating like mad. I imagined her planning and scheming, hiding underwear in strange places just like I'd done. Maybe when she kissed her husband it was like kissing Mike Tyler. Maybe she was waiting for the right time to come along when she'd do something. I watched the Ferris wheel circling and circling while Donnie ran the cushion over to his mother, and I felt like I might throw up myself. She looked over as Donnie was walking back to me and she lifted her hand, then she looked over at the shop booth where there was an engine recently reassembled by three guys in my class. Mr. Sinclair was there with his big foot propped up on the table. He was talking to some men but the whole time he was looking at her.

"Let's go," Donnie said suddenly, and I told him that we had to ride at least one ride so that I could tell my parents all about it without lying. He looked reluctant, his mind counting off every second it would take to drive out to the Royal Villa Inn, which was twenty miles away. Finally he gave in and bought two tickets for the Ferris wheel. When we stopped at the very top, our cart rocking back and forth, I could see Mr. Sinclair had made his way over and now was sitting right beside Donnie's mother.

"What was it you wanted to tell me?" Donnie asked. "You said you knew something funny."

"Well, not that I know something," I said and tried to force my brain to think a little faster while I watched Mrs. Wilkins begin to pack up her baked goods like she might be closing shop. It was at that moment I thought of Bill and how he was going to be out there in the parking lot, waiting. All I could think was that if the story got out it would all be my fault. Donnie would never forgive me, not to mention stop loving me. Then we would never have that perfect moment to take our clothes off.

"It's just an idea is all," I said. And then I told him that I had a fantasy of being with him in the *car*, that I'd fought it by saying again and again how cheap and meaningless I thought it was, but that really it was what I wanted more than anything. I said my biggest fantasy was being parked in that lot right behind my very own house. I knew as soon as the words left my mouth that I had ruined our night, that there was no way I'd be showing off my underwear; he moved his arm from around my shoulder and just sat there staring at me. We were stuck at the top again, and now his mother was standing with her purse over her shoulder. I couldn't believe he wasn't watching her, noticing something.

"It's pretty strange," he said. "But okay. I've heard girls have a lot of ideas about how the first time—" His sentence was cut short when the machine bolted and lurched forward, dropping us down and then lifting us back up. Scooter Clark was just a blur below as he bent to pick up something beneath the Bullet. When our cart was stopped on the ramp, our safety bar lifted, Donnie kissed me full on the mouth, then grabbed my hand and pulled me off towards Shoney's. He moved faster and faster until I had to run to keep up with him. I would have been excited out of my mind if all this other hadn't been going on. We passed Jennifer, who smiled and gave me the thumbs-up sign and then turned to whisper something to Rowland and Mike Tyler, who was standing close by. The story was starting;

like a match head struck against a rough surface, it had
leapt to life and now would begin spreading in and among
our classmates. I could almost see it happening, a trail of
words cutting through all the people, reaching all the ears
except those of my brother, who would already be out in
the parking lot, waiting.

Donnie was out of breath when we got to the car, and
just kept grinning at me in that way that made my heart
almost stop. He pulled me over beside him, his arm around
my shoulder while he drove with his left hand. When we
passed by my house, I could see Granddaddy sitting in the
living room, as motionless as the lamp beside him. Donnie
pulled into the far end of the lot, parked, and leaned over
to kiss me.

"Nervous?" he asked when he opened his eyes to find me
staring right back. "You're acting kind of weird."

"I am?" I asked, and he nodded, laughed.

"But that's okay," he whispered into my neck, his breath
warm on my skin as he fumbled with the buttons on my
sweater. I saw the bushes move, and I knew it was Bill and
his friends. They were smoking cigarettes; I could see the
flare of matches and the tiny red glows marking where they
huddled in the shrubbery. Donnie's mouth covered mine,
and I quickly pushed him away and moved to my side of
the seat. "Can't we talk a little first?" I asked.

"Sure." He tapped his finger on the steering wheel,
breathed in and out in puffs. It seemed the longer we were
quiet, the more rapid those puffs became. Once I saw Bill

peek in the window and then squat quickly; I was going to break his neck. I asked Donnie about his plans to go to Yale. How far was it to Connecticut anyway? Would he be taking a lot of courses? Did he think we'd date other people or keep on going together? How much snow would he see over the winter? Did he think he'd come home often or just on the major holidays? What did he think about the new Madonna video? Did he think his mama liked me or not? He answered everything politely but his answers were getting shorter and shorter, the last one a simple *yes*.

"Why didn't you just say you didn't want to go through with our plan?" he finally asked. I turned to face him and the moment I did, headlights circled and crossed his face. It was the Honda, lights cut as it moved slowly to the side of the lot opposite ours. It was *her*. I imagined how it all worked: Mr. Wilkins goes home and suddenly the evening is convenient after all. She makes a phone call. They are short-handed at the booths. Who can possibly come now that poor Mr. Wilkins is sick? Poor Mrs. Sinclair can't come. She can't get a babysitter on such short notice. Mr. Sinclair will just have to do it. And he says, "Aw, honey, I don't want to go. I have to deal with those crappy people all week long." But it's his duty and in no time there he is meeting his lover in the parking lot behind my house. Does he *really* like her or is he telling stories about how he'll die if they don't meet? Does he catch her in the school hallways and whisper *tonight is the night*?

Bill and his friends had put out their cigarettes and I

watched the shrubs move slightly as if by the wind, as the troop made its way around the lot.

"I'm sorry," I said to Donnie.

"So now what happens?" He was watching the car. I was watching Bill getting closer and closer.

"I don't know." I was too scared to cry. My mind was working so fast in so many directions that it was like it stopped functioning, and when I saw Mr. Sinclair's head-lights turning into the lot, I jumped out and began running toward the shrubs where Bill was hidden. I still don't know why I felt the need to keep everybody from knowing what they were up to, but I did. It seems like I was thinking about the way my parents looked at each other when they didn't know I was looking, a look that let me know they wanted to be together.

"What are you doing hiding in those bushes?" I kept yell-ing. "Can't a couple get a little privacy?" I ran right up beside Donnie's mama's window so that I blocked the sight of her, and immediately she cranked her car and screeched backwards. I turned and there was a slow second when I knew we were looking at each other, and then she was gone, almost sideswiping Mr. Sinclair along the way.

"Why'd you do that?" Bill stepped from the bushes, some-how looking older now that he had a group following him. "You messed it all up. They'll never come back now."

I heard a car door slam and then Donnie was walking across the parking lot. I looked to see if my parents were in the window but I couldn't tell. Bill turned and looked at me then. "What are you doing out here?"

"Same as you," I said, the words coming to me quickly. "We're out here spying."

"Yeah, right. That's why you scared them off." Bill was staring first at Donnie and then at my unbuttoned sweater that was hanging off one shoulder. My black lacy bra was showing. His friends were laughing, ready to spread the word. "What are you *really* doing?" Bill asked, his face red, from embarrassment or anger I wasn't sure.

"What do you think?" I asked, the words coming to me quickly. I turned and rubbed my hand up and down Donnie's chest, kissed him on the mouth. My legs were shaking like crazy. "So why don't you leave?" I looked at Bill the way I always looked at him, like he was scum and not worth my breath. "Go on."

"Why?"

"Because you're a jerk," I said, "and you're in our way." There was a brief flicker of feeling on his face, a hurt look that maybe I wouldn't have even noticed if we hadn't felt so close the night before. Now he had no choice but to get me back, to go along with his friends and spread some rumors, or at least to act like he had. "Donnie and I want to be alone . . ." I let my voice trail off with a lilt that implied a lot. Might as well let Donnie's reputation get some mileage out of it. It would be good for him. Boys would elbow him and nod knowingly. His mother would stare at him every morning and be left to wonder how much he knew and what we really did. It would keep her squirming for a long while.

My reputation was dirt by Monday morning, and even though Donnie still walked me to my classes we both knew things would never be the same. After all that teasing in front of Bill and his friends, I had gone back to the car and cried. I don't mean polite little sniffles either. I mean out-and-out sobs, the kind that leave you with red splotches all over and a stuffed-up head. Donnie said he didn't understand me at all. That he didn't think he could take much more of my leading him on. He said that if I was trying to *hook* him permanently, then we weren't thinking the same way. "I was," I told him. "I was trying to get it so you'd marry me." I thought later *that* was a dumb thing to have said; I mean, if he'd repeated *that* I wouldn't have had a date for the next century. But he didn't. As a matter of fact, he didn't say anything at all. Nothing. He made no effort to correct the rumors that we had *done it* five times in the back of his daddy's Chrysler, once under an old live oak at Hermit's Crossing, and yet another time in the Led Zeppelin Laser Light Show. Be real.

By the time graduation came around and I had spent two months as a *bona puella* with no dates at all, things died down a little. I spent most of my time with Bill, the two of us playing cards or talking while Granddaddy stared at us. There were so many nights when I almost told Bill the whole story, but I couldn't risk it. By then (despite her husband's differing opinion) Mrs. Wilkins had gone out of her way to show me all kinds of financial aid forms *just in case you might be interested, a smart young woman such as yourself.* We never *said* anything about what I knew but, as they say, a picture paints a thousand words and we were doing it all with our eyes. Mr. Wilkins watched her every move like he was waiting for a mistake. But the worst part of it all was the way my parents couldn't look me full in the face for a while.

Sometimes when I think about it all, I wish that I had never crept out that night while Bill was sleeping. Then I would've just gone on about my business, to the carnival and then out to the Royal Villa Inn, where I would've taken my clothes off. Donnie would've gone off to school and I would've stayed at home—not a virgin—and worked somewhere like Pick-a-Chick, ending my day with bunions and a polyester uniform that smelled of grease. I would have eventually gotten around to going to Tech; I would have had to take the long route. Would it have been worth it, that one thrilling moment? Sometimes I think maybe it would've because I loved Donnie Wilkins like I'd never loved anybody. Sometimes I still think about kissing him and imagine myself in black lingerie writhing on a bed like Madonna.

Instead, I was called into The Counselors' office one day late in the spring to be told that I had a full scholarship to the state university. "It was very lucky that there was an open spot this late in the year; I'm sure you'll do very, very well," Mrs. Wilkins said and handed me a letter that spelled it all out.

I wanted to say "mmmmm mmmmm mmmmm," as I looked over the letter but instead I said "thank you." Mr. Wilkins was standing there in all his Tinkertoy glory, acting like he was the one who had gotten it for me.

"Thank *you*," she said, and it was clear that she meant it. It was the first time she ever looked me square in the eye and smiled.

On graduation night, my scholarship and attendance to State were announced along with all the others (including Donnie's acceptance to Yale), and when I walked across the stage to get my diploma from Mr. Sinclair it seemed he held my hand a little longer and a little tighter than he had everyone else's. It was like a silent pact, this scholarship of mine. It was as binding as the one Donnie and I had made to each other even though we'd never seen it through. I looked up at the rows of seats in the auditorium until I found my parents and Bill, all three of them waving at me. I walked under those bright lights while Mr. Sinclair told the whole auditorium that I planned to go to State and become an architect. I figure I've got the rest of my life to fall in love and take my clothes off for a man, but I don't have so long to be my parents' future. I mean, someday they're going to be sitting there like Monterey Jack, staring at me with a blank empty look, and I want to know that I made at least one decision that was right.